Where No Ravens Fly

After a long hiatus following the death of his wife, Annie Blue, sometime Pinkerton Agent, Deputy US Marshal and freelance detective Lucas Santana is once again called to serve. The smooth-talking, well-read Wyoming private eye is ordered south to Riverton County Texas, to investigate the rumoured growing unrest there. Washington is worried that the ambitions of one man could destroy the peace on that lonely stretch of borderline.

The ambitious Frank Vagg controls the local law on both the Mexican side and the Texas side of the Rio Grande, straddled as it is by his headquarters, the township of San Pedro. Santana's attractive contact, Henri Larsson, wary at first of the senior operative with the reputation for action, proves to be more of a match than he would like. Santana attracts trouble like horse manure attracts dung beetles and it isn't too long before he is compelled to use his big Colt. When the lead begins to fly he is joined by fellow Pinkerton agents Joshua Beaufort and Jacob Benbow and the body count gro[...] grim, grey borderline county where no ravens fly.

Where No Ravens Fly

Harry Jay Thorn

A Black Horse Western

ROBERT HALE

© Harry Jay Thorn 2018
First published in Great Britain 2018

ISBN 978-0-7198-2715-0

The Crowood Press
The Stable Block
Crowood Lane
Ramsbury
Marlborough
Wiltshire SN8 2HR

www.bhwesterns.com

Robert Hale is an imprint
of The Crowood Press

The right of Harry Jay Thorn to be identified as
author of this work has been asserted by him
in accordance with the Copyright, Designs and
Patents Act 1988

Typeset by
Derek Doyle & Associates, Shaw Heath
Printed and bound in Great Britain by
CPI Group (UK) Ltd, Croydon, CR0 4YY

This one is for Harriet, Toby, Marta and Chris, the young ones who keep me on my toes, and for my friend David Wilmot, with many thanks for the lovely hand-crafted Rio Bravo Bowie knife, a super blade.

PROLOGUE

They prepared the shallow grave just as I had requested. They dug it near to Willard's Rock close by the small stream that chased the breeze down the mountain. They dug it close to the spot where we had often spent our afternoons picnicking and happily gazing down on our Wildcat Ranch. It was a cold Wyoming afternoon.

County Sheriff Gus Street, Mayor Halloran, US Marshal Harry Beaudine and Joshua Beaufort carried the narrow board upon which her body lay wrapped in a decorated shroud and lowered her gently to her rest. The undertaker's men filled in the grave and settled a large cairn of rocks over it to protect her body from foraging animals. Later, the blacksmith would come by and place the protective iron railing I had him forge around the grey stoned mound.

We were not regular churchgoers, but the Reverend Morris attended as a friend and led the singing of 'Shall we Gather at the River' and her long-time favourite song of the Civil War, 'Lorena'. A shaman from her tribe stepped forward and caressed the stones with eagle feathers and whispered the chant of the dead.

Later, the undertaker's assistant would bring the wooden marker bearing her name and settle it in the ground at the head of the grave. It would simply read: 'Annie Blue. Rest in Peace.' I had requested that no date be shown: Annie Blue was timeless.

When all was done, I thanked Halloran, the doc and Preacher Morris, and hobbled to our buggy. Gus helped me back up on to the seat and Bart, our dog, settled himself at my feet, making sure his shaggy head was within reach of my caressing hand. My leg was still very stiff and painful from an old wound, and my left shoulder ached constantly, the pain increased by the chill wind rising from the north and bringing with it little flurries of snowflakes. In order to remove the bullet lodged against the bone, which was thought to be a ricochet from the metal frame of our swing seat, Doc Evens had done some necessary digging to find it. The surgery was more damaging than the bullet wound. Annie had not suffered: the round had struck her in the heart and she had died there on the seat next to me while reaching for my falling body. Instantly: no time to even say goodbye.

Two rounds on an early winter's Saturday evening that would change my life forever.

For the most part, we drove in silence with Pinkerton agent Josh Beaufort and US Marshal Harry Beaudine riding close and silently on each side of us.

Passing the rocky outcrop from whence the shots had come, I asked quietly, 'Any news, Gus?'

The old lawman shook his head. 'We found two casings over there behind the highest rock, .44.40s. A carbine, we think, seeing as the range would have been too far for a handgun; even a marksman such as yourself would have been pushed with a Colt.'

'Dead end then?'

'Seems like it, the ground was chewed up and littered with horse shit so he had been watching the trail for some time. We followed the tracks back until they joined the Blackwater Pike, and there they joined with a hundred others and were lost. Your Sioux friend, Jimmy Eagle, spent days looking for some sign, some inkling of whichaway the shooter might have gone, but nothing.'

'So, it ends there?' I was not angry, I had nowhere, no direction in which to aim my anger but I was frustrated by the fact that, because of my wounds, I was counting on others to do what I was so good at. Finding people who had no wish to be found was my job.

'The Federals are on it, as are the Pinkertons. Something will turn up. You still don't have any thoughts on it yourself? No one you have annoyed lately, enough to make them want to kill you?'

'Like I told you and Beaudine, the last two were straightforward seek-and-find cases for Pinkerton, and the only other was for a private client: a petty thief and a wannabe bad man protection artist in Riverside who caved at the sight of me. All three were very minor and resolved without bloodshed. I haven't fired my gun in the line of duty for two years now, since that shootout in Peaceful when those damned drunken Montana wolvers knifed you and treed the town.'

'And before that?'

'West Texas, too far away and too long ago to be connected to this.' I spoke the words with a great deal of confidence, little realising how time and distance mean very little to a man filled with hate.

CHAPTER ONE

JOSHUA BEAUFORT

The hot afternoon sun burned through the large front office window, but the hot Texas air was quickly cooled by a large and innovative electric fan set in the high ceiling of the conference room. Pinkerton, although thrifty, spared no expense when it came to the comfort or security of his top detective squad.

Major Joshua Beaufort, once of the Southern Army of Virginia, was a long-time Pinkerton agent working for the big Scottish detective during the Civil War. He switched his allegiance from the Confederacy to the Union Army in one bold effort to save lives and, in so doing, perhaps shortened the war. In company with a young Union soldier Jacob Benbow, he had returned to Texas and brought about the demise of a smuggling racketeer, Buford Post, who had been fuelling the flames of war by supplying stolen Henry repeating rifles to the south. Thus, the bitter conflict could have continued at an even bloodier pace.

With the peace came other ventures, and his success had earned him the post of Agent in Charge of the San Antonio office and a meeting with Lucas Santana, sometimes known as the Peaceful River Kid. It was a quite meaningless sobriquet, Beaufort knew, and one Santana only used whenever his persona needed a mysterious lift. It was surprising what a made-up name could do for a man or woman in the unsettled and often untamed west: Wild Bill Hickock wasn't really wild, Sundance was a long way off being a kid and Mary Jane Canary was far from being calamitous.

Beaufort sat at the head of the large leather-topped table already littered with documents and, taking a large wad of papers from a bulky leather satchel, shook more of them onto the table in front of his companions: two of his top agents and a federal lawman. His second-in-command, Jacob Benbow, sorted them and Agent Larsson filed them under their relevant categories. US Marshal Harry Beaudine looked on with some amusement as the three shifted the papers around in some intelligible order, his own office usually being a nightmare of muddle.

'You got that, Henri?' Beaufort asked. Henri was the most used name for Henrietta Larsson, one of a growing number of female Pinkerton agents.

'It's all a bit of a mess, actually, Chief, but you know

what to expect from the Feds: the bigger the case, the greater the confusion, else they wouldn't need us.' She looked over at Beaudine. The big man gave her a sheepish grin and returned her green-eyed wink. The four had worked together on several occasions and were comfortable in each other's company. Besides, were he a younger man, and single, Harry Beaudine might have harboured thoughts that went beyond a working relationship, even at the risk of irritating his old friend, Josh Beaufort. She was a handsome woman, sure enough. Tall and straight without being rangy, short black hair and a masculine kind of face; square, yet somehow attractive on the woman. Dressed as usual in a white blouse and dark skirt, she looked exactly what she was: an efficient no nonsense detective. Her input was always welcomed and very much appreciated by the three lawmen.

'What more do you need?' Beaudine asked, after much of the paperwork had been digested and discussed by the trio. 'Your company is happy to take it on and the government are happy to pay for your services, but we do feel the need for some speed here before matters get out of hand.'

'The only more we need,' said Beaufort quietly, 'is a man on the inside, and I think I know just the man if we can talk him into it.'

'The same man I'm thinking of?' Beaudine asked quietly.

'None other.'

'Then you had best get on a train and head north.'

13

'Who are we talking about here?' Agent Henrietta Larsson asked, looking from one to the other.

'Lucas Santana,' Benbow chuckled. 'The Peaceful River Kid himself.'

The winter dragged by slowly for me. It took longer for my wound to heal than I had thought. I suspected my inner wound, the loss of my lovely wife, would never heal. Out of necessity I hired an old wrangler, Jesse Overlander, who I had known since the time I had first moved to Blackwater County, to run the Wildcat for me. I told him to take on help if he needed it, as it would be a long while before I would be of any real use. He was an amiable middle-aged man, a fair country cook and good company on the long dark evenings when the demons and the whiskey took a hold of me. Bart approved him, so he moved in to the small but comfortable cabin I had had built for just such a purpose, should hired help ever be needed. With close on five hundred head of prime Wyoming beef and more on the way, I guessed that extra help would have been needed following a long spring and a mild winter, even in happier circumstances.

I pondered long and hard while my wounds healed, seeking answers I could not find. Beaufort's enquiries had rendered nothing new and Harry Beaudine, fully occupied with problems across the state, had admitted it had been pushed to one side and would remain there unless any new information was received. The reward money I offered for that information was never claimed, and as the winter passed, so did my hope of ever finding the lone gunman who had robbed me so cruelly of my Annie Blue.

And so it was and late.

One early spring evening I was alone in the barn tending to the ranch milk cow. Annie had named her Susan, for some obscure reason, and the big animal was about to give birth. Her bellowing must have drowned out his approach, since the first I knew of his arrival was a loud cough. I turned, reaching automatically for the gun that was not there. I seldom wore a sidearm on the ranch but old habits die hard, or range detectives do not make old bones.

'Are you ready to get back to work, Lucas, or are you going to spend the rest of your days with your arm stuck up a cow's backside?' Pinkerton agent Joshua Beaufort stood in the open doorway with a wide grin on his darkly moustachioed handsome face.

I turned my back on Susan and walked towards him, offering him my hand. He graciously declined, stepping smartly back, and the smile turned to laughter.

'Come up to the house. She can wait. Probably better off without my interfering, anyways.'

I led the way past his buggy and stopped at the water tank to wash Susan's insides from my arms and hands.

'You play nursemaid to every cow you have, personal like?'

'No, only old Susan; she's more of a pet, gives us our daily milk and, once in a while, a very sellable lady calf.'

The Wildcat headquarters were not grand, but both comfortable and homely at the same time. It contained Indian rugs, two large bookcases, a gun rack, dining table and leather chairs in the larger room set in front of the big open fireplace, and two bedrooms and a kitchen with an indoor bathroom built to Annie's specifications. It was clean and tidy; no real thanks to me, but to Jesse's sister who came by once a week to smooth things over, change the linen and clear out the fireplace. She also cooked us both a meal that was the best grub of the week.

Beaufort stepped past me and picked up the silver-framed sepia-toned photograph of Annie and me that stood atop the piano I had imported from Cheyenne. 'Lovely lady, Lucas; not sure she would be in favour of you sitting on your backside all winter and spring.'

I shrugged. 'Leg still aches a little in the cold from that hit I took in Peaceful a while back.'

'Arm seems well enough to fit a cow's ass, and there's no limp now that I can see. Gus Street tells me you ride well enough. Also, you are getting a mite thick around the belly.'

'Have you eaten?' I asked, ignoring all comments.

'Not since a late breakfast in Peaceful.'

'There's a bottle on the table. Help yourself, and I'll get Jesse to take care of the buggy. I guess you will be staying the night?' I said, hopefully.

'Maybe a couple; I need a break. Things are pretty hectic in Texas at the moment, but my deputy can handle most of what comes his way.'

'Deputy? You have a deputy now?' I took out the makings from my shirt pocket and rolled a neat cigarette. He declined my offer of loose tobacco, preferring instead a tailor-made smoke from a leather cigarette case.

'Not a deputy in the lawman sense, but as in a second-in-command; it's just a word, really.'

'Let me guess,' I said, 'Jacob Benbow?'

'That's the word.'

'Top man,' I said, remembering the young Yankee from a couple of past encounters: one in West Texas and one right here in Peaceful. During both, he had made the difference between life and death for the pair of us in two horrendous shootouts. 'He still tote that Henry rifle?'

'Never without it.' He crossed the room to my gunrack, looked at me for my nod of approval, and carefully removed the rifle he had presented me with at the successful closure of the first case we had ever worked together. 'Lovely piece, the Henry. "Load it on Sunday and shoot all week long", isn't that what they used to say? Sixteen rounds of hell. Not so popular now, though; most lawmen carry the Winchester .44.40. I guess it's easier if you have a saddle gun that fires the same centre fire ammunition as your sidearm.'

I put the coffee pot on the small iron stove that served to warm the kitchen and dining area. 'I guess so,' I said.

He set the rifle back on the rack and turned to me,

17

the smile gone replaced by a soulful sadness. 'I am so sorry, Lucas, so sorry we could not do more. We tried. . . Believe me, we tried every which way, but nothing, not even a hint. Even with the reward, nothing.'

I turned to him. 'I know you did, Josh, both of you. Even with Beaudine's office helping. It's just one of those things we will never know. In our line of work, we cross many trails. Some are long, some are short and many lead us nowhere. Who knows what rocks we turn over in our passing? When you bring a man down you never can tell how many you bring down with him, like ripples from a pebble in a lake, too many to count. You did your best, all of you did that for Annie, and I am obliged, but what is done is done. . . .'

'As Lady Macbeth once said,' he interrupted me. The smile returned to his sunburned Texas face, lifting the darkness which had briefly settled around us. 'I know you are well-read.'

'Damned right, I am,' I said.

'We have a case for you. Might be a tough one, could be a long one but better than punching cows all summer and putting your hand where no man's hand should ever be put.'

I felt that tingle, that little stirring of expectation, that promised whisper of action, of doing what some folk thought I was born to do, but I kept those thoughts to myself as I rolled another smoke and feigned disinterest. Beaufort waited, and I waited, and the silence between us grew until we both burst out laughing. It was the first real laughter heard on Wildcat for a long while.

'Manhunt?' I asked, killing the laughter.

'More than that, Lucas, it could be one of the biggest cases Pinkerton has ever handled for the Feds. Big trouble coming to south Texas. You are familiar with Texas, are you not?'

We shared more laughter.

CHAPTER TWO

THE PEACEFUL
RIVER KID

I had spent the best part of an hour drinking with Beaufort and listening to the outline of a case undertaken jointly by the attorney general's office and the Pinkerton Detective Agency before the subject of my unfortunate sobriquet came up.

'Where the hell did you get that moniker, Lucas? You sure enough are not a kid; doubt that you ever were.'

I stared up at the ceiling, thinking while looking through the smoke hanging in the wooded roof. 'It was a while back. You ever hear tell of an Arizona gunfighter called One-Eyed Jack Temple?'

'Sounds familiar. A while back since I heard tell of him, though.'

'Well, one time I was in a poker game in Cheyenne and it turned ugly. Only five us in the game: three hard-assed no-account yahoos and this big old one-eyed man with a black patch over his right eye. I was holding good hands, and it turned real nasty and ill tempered when I scooped in the pot on a bluffed and very busted flush. The only bad hand I had all evening and it was still a winner.'

'Not always good to be a winner, I guess.' Beaufort examined the contents of his near empty glass and refilled it.

'It looked real dark there for a minute or two when this gent pipes in, his voice little more than a whisper and his words precise, and asks me, "Say, boy, are you not the mean sonofabitch they call the Peaceful River Kid?" I just stare at him and he goes on, "The *hombre* that shot and killed dead the Yancy brothers up around Wyoming someplace, as I recall?"

'The poker players went dead quiet and he fixed me with that one obsidian black eye. I let my coat fall open so them assholes could see my shoulder rig and the fancy Colt .32 Rainmaker snugged away there. I did not answer the old man with but a slight nod of my head, and those boys settled down real friendly like and quit the game soon after.

'Later, I met the old man at the bar and bought him a drink or two before asking him who the hell the Peaceful River Kid was. Again, he fixed me with that one twinkling eye and says, "I guess you are now, my friend. It is surely strange; you add the word kid onto

21

a fellow's name and he sure enough becomes someone to walk around."

'I offered him my hand and told him I was Louis Bassett out of Wichita, a name I sometimes use. The original Bassett was a friend of mine, a lawman of some repute. He taught me how to shoot and, more importantly, when not to pull. He was working as a part time deputy and he took a blast from a sawed-off shotgun fired from an alleyway in Dryburg, New Mexico. A deadbeat named Sy Randolph bragged on the killing and he was later found shot to death in a dry wash outside of the town limits. He was buried in a shallow grave with a sawed-off for a marker, barrels in the sand and his hat on the cut down stock. His killer was never apprehended.'

Beaufort looked at me long and hard. 'That a true story, Lucas?'

'Yes, it is, hand of God and you can take that to the bank. I use it now and again just to see if it still has any currency, and it appears so.'

'You know who gunned down this Randolph character?'

I ignored the question, and I fired and drew deeply on the cigarette in the long silence that followed.

'And the old man, this One-Eyed Jack Temple,' Beaufort eventually broke that silence. 'You ever see him again?'

I shook my head. 'Never saw him again after that night, but I guess he's still out there somewhere.'

He waited some more, then asked, 'You carry a

Rainmaker? I heard they are unreliable.'

'They can be in double action, but I had mine worked on by Art Brewer in Cheyenne. He's a master gunsmith and friend of Harry Beaudine. He hand-forged some new parts and it works like a dream; never had a misfire yet. It's slim and tucks away without revealing itself. Pretty, too.'

'I would like to see it later, top man is our Art, did he cut down that big old Sharps on your rack for you?'

'Yes, took that from a trigger-happy Montana wolfer I caught trespassing on Wildcat. It makes it a fine saddle gun.'

'Do you fancy a return visit to south Texas, Lucas?'

It came out of the blue. I thought about that for a minute or two before replying, 'Josh, did you ever wonder why queens and kings of hearts, spades and the jack of clubs have two eyes and the poor old king of diamonds and the jacks of hearts and spades only have the one?'

He shook his head. I let it hang there a moment or two and said, 'Me neither.'

CHAPTER THREE

SOUTH TEXAS AGAIN

Beaufort, as always, was passionate and convincing, making me believe everything he said but, deep down, I knew he was very uncertain about that of which he spoke. I guessed if it had been clear-cut they would not have called me in. It wasn't that I was expendable, it was because my methods were a little more direct and sometimes a tad beyond the law; so much so that there was paper on me in some states and a county warrant or two besides.

'It isn't exactly the south Texas, you know, but there-abouts, and well below the New Mexico border and close enough to the Rio to spit across the line,' Beaufort said.

'Country is much the same: unfriendly, hot and

often dry, rocky and with a sky filled with ravens,' I said.

'New Mexico and Texas border country: sounds about right. There is a small, no-account town down there on our side that is around half the size of the one on the Mex side. It's complicated.'

'Its name?' I asked.

'That's another part of the problem. It's called San Pedro on both sides, which only adds to the confusion. Our side was once a gold town that never happened. It dried up and died before it was born. Their side is bandit country: Yaqui, the worst kind, and a no-go area to us by order of the US Attorney's office. Hence, Beaudine cannot go in there and we don't really have an agent with your Mexican experience to work it.'

He was referring to the fact that, on several occasions, I had crossed the border to apprehend a fugitive without papers from the Mexican authorities. Some called it kidnapping. But me, I saw it as a job, and the Rio Grande as just another river to cross.

'So, why is this one a problem to the US? Sounds a pretty familiar story all along the border, where those towns were once part of Mexico anyway.'

'Truth to tell, Lucas, we do not know.' He sounded apologetic.

'You don't know? So why the hell are you passing it down the line to me?'

'We have heard tell of unrest down there from Tad Jones, the sheriff of Patterson County. He's based in Sentinel, the nearest law. The US part of San Pedro is actually in Riverton County and is a no-account town twenty miles or so to his south, but well within our borderline.'

'Unrest?' I didn't care too much for that word.

'Random killings, rustling, illicit trade in alcohol and God knows what else. General lawlessness, more so on the Mex side of San Pedro than on our side, but Washington does not want it to spread north more than it already has. Bottom line is, I guess, the railroad is headed that way and the US Government has a good deal of money invested in that enterprise through various companies. Too much to ignore, but not enough to do too much about. Things are a mite strained with Mexico at present, as you know. Troopers appearing down there would raise a hell of a lot of dust, so to speak.'

'Could be a land grab,' I offered. 'Wouldn't be the first time news of a possible railroad has triggered such a move. Lot of government money to be made from real estate on a right of way.'

Beaufort shrugged. 'Maybe so, but Beaudine thinks it may be more than that, and he needs to be sure before he runs any obvious interference with the local law.'

'Fee or wages?' I asked.

'Same set-up as usual: your fee and anything you can legally make on the side.'

'And exactly what do you want of me?'

'Well, to be clear, there could well be a little more to this caper than just a land grab. We have codenamed it Operation Diablo.'

'Colourful,' I said.

'I thought so.'

'Why Diablo?'

'It's a whispered word a couple of our agents have picked up. They work undercover with the great and the good, the banking set of San Antonio. We do not know exactly what it means, but every case needs a name, so Benbow gave it that one.'

'Imaginative lad, that corporal.'

'Not so much a lad anymore, Lucas; a man full grown in every way. A little hasty at times, but one hundred per cent reliable.'

'You want me down in south Texas right away?'

'Yes, the sooner the better. Go see Tad Jones in Sentinel. He's not a man to exaggerate a situation; he can only observe as it is out of his bailiwick. Go down there, get a feeling for it, and check out a man named Frank Vagg, a local bigshot. Get back to me in San Antonio so that we can assess the problem and find a solution, if one is actually required. I've seeded the mine some for you,' he smiled. 'It may be all smoke in the wind, but we have the job through Beaudine and, all things considered, we think you are the man for the job.'

'Why me, exactly?'

'The usual reasons. You think outside of the rules. You're not tall, and not short; not fat and not skinny; your age is undetermined. You are a chameleon, a shadow; you fit in and yet you don't; and you speak a little Spanish.'

'And I'm expendable?'

'You know better than that, Lucas. No Pinkerton man is expendable.'

'Will I be working alone?'

'No, not exactly: we already have an agent in San Pedro setting things up for you.'

'Benbow?' I asked.

'Hell no,' he grinned, 'Agent Henri Larsson.'

'Henry Larsson? A good man?'

'Not a man; that's Henri with an "i", as in Henrietta.'

'A woman?'

'I do believe so.'

'A Dutchy?' I asked.

Beaufort nodded.

'Didn't turn out too well for the last female agent I worked with, did it?'

It was not really a question.

He smiled sadly. 'No, it didn't, but we have moved on some since then.'

'Taught them to dodge a bullet?'

'I know you blame yourself for her death, Lucas, but you should not. Line of duty deaths are inevitable in our kind of work, for men or women. We know the odds and you brought her killer to justice. It's all we can hope to do.'

'She was a bonny lady,' I said, not wanting to go back to the day an agent named Kathleen Riley took rounds in the back from a hired gun when we had gotten a little too close to his employer.

'She sure enough was, and the department has grown. You don't get to carry a Pinkerton shield unless you are able and willing to take that risk.' He raised his glass. 'To Kathleen,' he said, and we drank the bottle dry, each lost in his own thoughts.

That night, I lay on my bunk listening to the breeze ruffling the leaf-laden branches of the live oak out back of the ranch house. It was where I had built the swing seat for Annie and me to sit and grow old together. Of course, in my line of business, it would never have worked out that way. We'd be sitting there one day, and the next my bedroll would be packed and I would be off somewhere, sometimes long gone and faraway. But I always came back, and she never tried to change me in any way, hoping, I supposed, that the times spent at home with her on Wildcat would grow. I fancied for a brief moment, as I drifted off to sleep, that I heard her gentle voice softly whispering *Lorena*, the old Civil War song, to me from faraway, her voice carried by that Wyoming breeze.

CHAPTER FOUR

SHAVE AND A HAIRCUT SIX BITS

The long train ride to San Antonio was only a shade more comfortable than the Overland stage ride to Sentinel for a short stay and briefing from old-time sheriff Tad Jones. He was as Beaufort described him: a no-nonsense lawman intent on keeping his county line clear of any possible trouble. He confirmed his report to Beaudine that he had nothing firm to offer, other than the fact that a man named Frank Vagg called the shots in San Pedro and that he was not a very approachable man, he's surrounded at all times by a personal bodyguard, and his ranch by a bevy of pistoleros; hired guns, mostly. They were men he considered to be border trash, but nevertheless men to be reckoned with. They were paid top dollar and were ready to earn it if needs be. He did not know too much of Vagg and had never met the man. Other than the fact he had been around for some years working a dubious trade across the Mexican border defined by the Rio Grande, he was something of an enigma.

Vagg was, by all accounts, a frail and elderly man, running San Pedro both south and north of the Rio. The Riverton County sheriff, one Billy Hunt, was Vagg's man, although there was little call for a lawman in San Pedro. Word had it that Vagg was the law, and any wrongdoer in his eyes tended to disappear. Jones was not judgemental, saying only that it would not be the way he would run the town were he the county law there. He bought me fine supper, and we shared a drink or two and memories of better days.

The next morning I was back on the Overland stage, San Pedro bound.

For a 'no-account town' as described by Beaufort, San Pedro was larger than I had been led to believe. A tree-lined Main Street, a bank, a saloon, billiard hall, two hotels, the drovers club, a large livery stable and corral, general store, blacksmith's shop, newspaper and Wells Fargo office, real estate office and, dominating the far end of Main Street, a well-maintained white painted church. Many of the business premises appeared to be constructed from freshly painted lumber. Even the Overland office, which also served as a post and telegraph office, did not fit the description given me of a dead or dying gold camp.

I have always found the most information gathered is either from a bartender or from a barber working on your head, irritatingly feeling the need to talk, even if you were not much in the mood to listen. However, in this case, I was. It was a small shop tucked away between a hardware store and the undertaker's: Harry's Barber Shop, its red and white pole faded in the Texas sun. The sign said, 'shave and a haircut six bits, two bits extra for a hot towel'. The barber was, as most of them seem to be, almost bald, with a wisp of hair clinging to the top of his bony head and a scattering of grey at the back and sides. It gave his head a white-framed skull-like appearance. He was skinny, round shouldered, with pale blue eyes and wore wire-rimmed spectacles. There were two chairs and no customers, so I walked in, hung my hat on the hat rack and my pistol belt beside that, within easy reach of the nearest chair.

'You Harry?' I asked, making it clear I was happy to jaw a while.

'No, sir, I'm Ben. Harry got himself shot last fall.'

'He give someone a bad haircut?'

'No, sir; Harry was a lot of things but he was great barber. Bad taste in women is all. Picked the wrong one and she shot him dead. Now doing ten to fifteen in the state Pen.'

'So, it looks like you are short one barber?' I said, nodding to the two chairs.

'No, sir, short of customers is all. What will it be: haircut or shave?'

I looked at my reflection in the cracked mirror. 'Both,' I said.

'That'll be a dollar even if you want the hot towel.' He waited seemingly expecting an objection.

'Just a trim around the ears and the back on the hair. Leave the moustache be when you shave.'

'That will still be a dollar even,' he repeated.

'Fine,' I said, and settled back in the chair as he draped a white cloth around me and tucked the back in just below the hairline. 'Kind of quiet for a border town.'

'Most of the action is across the river on the Mex side. You can get a haircut, a shave and get your bell rung for a dollar down there.'

'It looks to be a busy town to me.'

'Look closer. You will see the newspaper office is closed; permanent, I guess. The millinery and the attorney's office are very part-time and the jail is usually empty. The undertaker is busy, though, and the church is full of hypocrites come Sunday morning.'

He spent a couple of minutes snipping at thin air to make me think I was getting my silver dollar's worth, and then brushed the debris from my collar. He placed a towel on my chest, lathering up my face and stropping the open razor.

'You come far?' he asked.

'Far enough.'

'You going far?'

I didn't answer. I don't like moving my lips when an open bladed razor is scraping away at my jaw.

He was gentle and efficient, wiping my face with a warm towel and rubbing something that burned; it smelled vaguely like horse liniment on my cheeks.

'Anything else I can do for you, sir?'

I looked at the shelf to where a closed jar held some red and white hard rock candy sticks.

He followed my gaze. 'It's for the kids. Keeps them quiet while I cut. Never understood why kids don't like to get their hair cut.'

'I'll take a stick,' I said. 'Don't much like getting my hair cut, either.'

He smiled, reached up for the jar, unscrewed the lid and shoved two sticks into a paper bag. 'They will cost you two bits; free to the kids, but you should know better.'

I gave him two dollars and told him to keep the change. I set my hat on my head and strapped on my gun-belt, settling the holster on the left side of my belly with the ivory grips forward.

I knew it was coming. 'Fancy rig,' he said. 'You a lawman?'

'No,' I said.

'Just as well; we already got a county sheriff. It's a small county and he don't need a deputy here. He's got one up at Riverton, the county seat, but he prefers to be down here. Fishing's better. Most of the time, like me, he has trouble finding something to do other than arrest a few busted drunks when we need Main Street cleaned of horse shit for free.'

'That would be?'

34

'Billy Bob Hunt. Been elected three times in a row.'

'And across the river?'

'They got their own law over there. Mexicans have little respect for federal law but they keep it south of the river, mostly. And when they don't, old Billy Bob goes fishing for crappies up at Springwater Creek. Clear water there before it reaches the big river.'

'You know a good place to eat?'

'Mostly Mex food and mostly hot. Not your thing? Then try the Blue Parrot. It's a restaurant out back of the Wayfarer's Hotel. Food's mostly good and the hotel is clean if you are staying a while.'

'And a quiet waterhole?'

'Well, there is a bar in the Wayfarer's and the only other one this side of the river is the Red Diamond down the end of the street, just short of the jail. If you were a respectable cattleman you could use the drovers club, but I do not think you are.'

I gave him my practised deadeye look and he flushed.

'A drover, I mean.'

I smiled, thanked him, resettled my hat and walked back out into the sunshine, across Main Street to the livery, and set about hiring a horse for a few days. I had no idea as to how many those days might be, but I didn't want to rent an animal chosen in haste, one I couldn't handle. Stock would need careful scrutiny before I put it between my legs. Big horses worry me, and I did not believe San Pedro would have a Morgan to rent . . . but I was wrong there.

CHAPTER FIVE

BILLY BOB HUNT

I registered for a room at the Wayfarer's Hotel and signed the book as Louis Bassett of Wichita, noting as I did so that Henrietta Larsson of San Antonio was there six days ahead of me. I had a wash, changed my clothes and made arrangements with the desk clerk to have my dirty gear picked up and laundered. It was quite a sophisticated burg for such a no-account small town, and I wondered where the influence for the comforts of the Wayfarer originated.

Like a lot of hot places, south Texas could burn you to death during the day and freeze the *cojones* off you when the sun went down. In the hotel diner, I sat as near as possible to the large potbellied stove as I could. Supper was good; Ben the barber had been right. I had steak, well cooked, with beans and baked potatoes and sat back warming my hands around a steaming mug of hot coffee.

Then he came, as I knew he would: sometimes the law can be as predictable as sunrise.

Sheriff Billy Bob Hunt was an elderly, short and rotund man in a frayed and well-worn tan three-piece wool suit, the buttoned vest adorned by a silver watch chain and a polished nickel star. His bright eyes belied his age, set deep in a tanned face lined like old leather, grey hair poking out beneath a tan derby hat. His smile was wide and his handshake firm. 'Mind if I join you for coffee, Mr Bassett?'

'No, sir,' I said and waved him to a seat opposite me.

'Welcome to our peaceful little community, and whatever your business here is, I hope you enjoy your stay, be it brief or long. If you are passing through, then I would suggest north rather than south. Mexico is having one of its fretful little turns at present and the border is not as it should be.'

He smiled a genuine, white-mouthed smile, and as much as it reminded me of a 'gator eying up its next meal, I had the feeling he really was just trying to be friendly. He offered me a stogie and I accepted it, looking directly into his eyes as I took a light from his match.

'Just one small thing, Mr Bassett.' He reached into his inside pocket and took out a folded sheet of paper, unfolded it and spread it out on the table, smoothing the creases as he did so.

It was a good likeness. It was a federal Wanted dodger. The Peaceful River Kid wanted in Patterson

County for questioning regarding the aggravated felonious assault on a federal officer of the law. So, this what was what Beaufort was smiling about when he said he had 'seeded the mine'.

'Not a bad likeness,' I said, 'but I wouldn't be seen dead in a hat like that, and I was never six feet tall.'

That alligator smile again. 'What the hell is aggravated felonious assault doing way out here? Assault is assault; how can it be anything but aggravated?'

I shrugged, pulled on my smoke and waited.

'Patterson County is out of my jurisdiction but they've got a good man down there in Tad Jones. He wants you; no doubt he will hear you are here and come get you if the ride is worthwhile, and I doubt that it is. We still don't hold federal law in any great stead down here.'

'I am sure he would, Sheriff Hunt. I am pretty sure he would.'

He studied on my answer for a long moment and said, 'Several strangers in town at present. Unusual this time of year. . . . Not part of some religious gathering, are you?'

'You serious?'

'No,' he laughed, 'not really, just so long as you're not about to start a war, you are welcome to San Pedro.'

'No war, no revolution and no bibles, I promise you. Just passing through is all, and needed a rest.'

He got to his feet, smiled again and turned to leave, turning back just as reached the door. 'You like fishing, Mr Bassett? If so, you come by and see me and I'll show you a little touch of paradise in this sun-baked Godforsaken county.'

CHAPTER SIX

THE LOOP

I read in a book somewhere that there is a plant that stinks so bad that only big blue-tailed flies can smell it. It attracts the biggest and the best, and once they have wandered inside of the thing they are never see again. I sometimes think I am the human equivalent to that plant in the way I attract attention from some of my fellow human beings. Life is a loop – mine seems to be, anyway – and I knew it would not be long before that blue-tail fly sought me out.

The following day, after a long and uneventful rest, I finished my evening meal of a well-cooked steak and baked potatoes awash in a sea of onion gravy. I tipped the attractive waitress far too generously, thanked her for lighting my stogie and made my way out of the Blue Parrot, through the hotel lobby and onto Main

Street. It was a little after nine and the smoky coal oil lamps were spluttering in the cool evening breeze that drifted up from the distant Rio Grande. It was too early for bed and there had been no contact with Henrietta Larsson. Maybe she was not aware of my arrival, so I used that thinking as my excuse for drifting down the street and into the Red Diamond saloon.

There were maybe a dozen customers seated or standing in the smoky gloom, one being Billy Bob Hunt playing dominoes with another elderly gent. He looked up and nodded, but that was all.

I bellied up to the bar and ordered a beer without a head. The barkeep glared but said nothing. I picked up a week-old copy of the *San Antonio Times*, which I guessed had been left by a fellow traveller, took out my spectacles and settled myself down for a quiet read of it.

And so the loop began.

Careful not to catch his eye, I studied the man in the long bar mirror. He was a big man, bulging belly but slim of hip and small of feet. He looked a bit like a kid's whipping top. He wore a dark brown suit over a white collarless shirt. His derby hat was propped on the back of his head and the deep-set eyes were filled with fire. He was arguing horse prices with a wizened little man in similar attire but, unlike the big man, he did not wear a sidearm as far as I could see. The big man was packing a Colt .45 SA Army in a tied-down tan leather holster. I studied on the paper but could not help but be aware of the harshly raised voice of the big

41

man. Unhappy with the lack of response from his small companion, he cast his eyes around the smoky room and settled them upon me, just as I was looking in the mirror and wondering why old Billy Bob paid no heed to the growing ruckus that any lawman worth his salt would have been on to in a heartbeat.

The loop, the stinking plant and the blue-tail fly.

'You,' the big man said, 'stranger, can I buy you a drink?' He moved away from his companion, his fire-lit eyes focusing on me.

'No, thank you, sir,' I said, 'I only ever have the one.'

'Where you from, friend?'

I took off my reading spectacles and placed them in their soft leather case, carefully folded the newspaper and finished my drink.

'You hear me, old man, or are you deaf as well as blind?'

There is no escaping the loop.

'I am neither, sir, but if you are really interested in my origins, I am from just about anywhere.'

He thought about that for a moment, shuffling a step or two down the bar. I was aware that the dominoes were no longer clicking and the barkeep had disappeared.

'You're the stranger in town. Rumour is you are on the dodge, is that right?'

'Don't believe all you hear. A rumour is just that: a rumour.'

'Do you know who I am?'

'No,' I said, 'and I am not that much interested, either.'

'Jimmy the Deuce.'

'Colourful,' I said. 'And now that we are acquainted, I think it to be my bedtime.' I stepped away from the bar, as did he.

'You any good with that fancy rig you're wearing?'

'Better than most,' I said, 'and far too good for you, Jimmy the Deuce.' It was a baiting remark but I was tired and, whatever I said, nothing was going to leave the loop open.

He stepped away from the bar and let his coat fall open. I heard a scraping of chairs behind me as customers got out of the line of any possible fire. I wondered if one of them was Sheriff Billy Bob Hunt . . . or had he already gone fishing? What to do? Perhaps it was time I got noticed; nothing travels faster than the news of a gunfight.

Jimmy was thinking, I supposed, of a smart reply and not coming up with one pulled. He was fast, but not fast enough by a long shot. The muzzle of his Colt was barely clear of the leather before he was looking down the barrel of mine. He froze.

'I told you so, Jimmy the Deuce, but you don't listen so good, do you?' It wasn't much of a question and I did not expect an answer, so I dropped the hammer and capped a round, blowing off most of his right ear. He screamed, dropped his gun and held his hand to his ruined ear, the blood dripping through his fingers. His little companion stared at me, not quite sure he believed what had just happened.

'You got a sawbones in town?' I addressed the question directly to him, raising my voice a little above the moaning of the crumpled Jimmy the Deuce. He nodded. 'Then get him there, pronto, before he bleeds to death.'

The barkeep reappeared and helped the little man and his weeping companion out through the swing doors.

I flipped open the loading gate of my Colt, put it to half cock and, turning the cylinder to the spent brass, rodded it clear and replaced it with a live round. I placed the spent casing on the bar. 'Souvenir,' I said quietly to the white-faced barkeep. 'Remember you had the Peaceful River Kid in here this evening.' I smiled the words but he remained white-faced.

And the loop was closed one more time.

The air stank of black powder smoke and my ears were ringing. Billy Bob Hunt walked over to me. 'Buy you a drink?'

'Why not?' I said.

'Two beers, Larry, and no heads.'

'Shouldn't you have stepped in there somewhere, Sheriff?' I said.

'Maybe so, but I was curious to see how you made out. You would not have been the first *pistolero* Jimmy Olds put in the ground. You did OK, but Jimmy was one right-hand man to Frank Vagg, who's a big shot around these parts, so watch your back.'

'Thanks for the warning.'

'Not so much a warning; more by the way of advice. As for not stepping in? That's easy: I believe you are going to be trouble to me. Jimmy is always trouble to me, so either way it went would have been a win-win situation for me.' He gave me the alligator smile and walked away carrying his beer, and pretty soon the dominoes were clicking again.

Some town, San Pedro.

CHAPTER SEVEN

FRANK VAGG

The Rio Grande was running low, an ideal time to cross the border and see to it that his interests in the Mexican side of the river were under control. A horseman could cross without getting his boots wet, but when it was running high in the rainy season, it was a swim. Not that Frank Vagg ever rode a horse across the river: he had a boat and an oarsman to carry his lightweight frame across. Frank Vagg did not like horses and he did not readily take to the border country, but it so suited his purpose in life, which was to make money. It was a boundary he could cross whenever he chose. It was a border that would, he suspected, forever be a gateway of hope to the Mexicans and a thorn in the side of the United States of America.

Vagg felt his position to be safe, and he was comfortable with men he trusted to ensure his well-being.

46

With troubled New Mexico to the north, Chihuahua to the south and the border town of El Paso to his west, he felt certain that if the railway came, it would come San Pedro's way. He heard a whisper that the government were staking money on it, so it stood to reason, he thought, that his money should follow theirs.

Although border conflict was rare, minor irritations were always apparent. But both sides offered lucrative rewards and San Pedro was highly suited for just about any game in town. The possibility of the Denver and Rio Grande railroad cutting west from Abilene and reaching this far down was a gift from heaven – if he believed in such a place, which he did not. He believed in very little beyond his own controlling influence backed by US coin. He was a grey cadaver of a man, a pale skull of a face with a short white goatee. He had a malnourished look about him that belied the energy he could muster in a crisis, and there had been many such moments in his life. His crumpled white suit hung loosely upon his bones, and the wide brim of his Panama straw protected his balding, liver-spotted scalp from the sun in the daytime and the coolness of the night, and rested on his large ears.

Frank Vagg sat his rocking chair and watched the misty evening draw in around him, the air filled with the night sounds of the wetlands and the river. He could smell it: that muddy smell filled with promise. He could hear it: the crickets, the night birds and the bullfrogs. Once he thought he heard the distant scream of a cougar but was not sure; from south of the

47

river many sounds drifted up to the front porch of his large adobe ranch house, and not all of it from the wildlife. The men he commanded in south San Pedro, mostly brutal renegade Yaqui who bore no allegiance to Mexico or the US, were far removed from those he employed on the Texas side of the river. He drew on his cigar and contemplated the day. It had not been a day that had filled him with pleasure. Jimmy Olds, one of his most trusted men, had gotten the best part of his right ear shot off by some drifter and he thought he had heard one of the many songs of the raven that morning.

Frank Vagg hated ravens with a passion. He considered them birds of ill omen and always had, from way back when he was a youngster in the Big Thicket country on the Arkansas border. He had seen two large, black birds pecking at the eyes of the dead cattle strewn across the dry grassland of his father's two-by-four ranch. Ravens were a rare sight in that part of the country: a migrating pair, he assumed. He did not blame the drought for the death of the cattle, nor for the death of his father, who had shot himself in the head following the death of that last steer. He did not blame the god his father had worshipped and trusted. He blamed the raven; it was the only tangible thing to hate. The raven feasted on the hate within him. His mother had died giving birth to his sister Margaret so, alone, the pair of orphans had been shipped off to an aunt and uncle in Virginia to be abused, beaten and raised as a duty without love or compassion. As a teenager, the young Frank Morris, a surname he later changed to Vagg, had killed them both with a stolen English sawed-off shotgun and fled with his young sister in tow. They disappeared – 'gone to Texas', as the saying went. It was a saying he was very fond of.

Ravens were filthy birds and were everywhere throughout this rocky landscape he called home. But no ravens flew above the Circle V. He had placed a handsome bounty on their black hides. At first it had been an easy bounty to earn, but not so now; the raven was, as much as he hated the thought, a smart bird and quickly learned where the boundaries of the ranch were and tended not to stray across the land where so many of their kin had disappeared. *They were in for a bit of a shock.* He smiled at the thought: the Circle V was set to expand.

The Yaqui he employed had done and continued to do an excellent job, crossing the border, firing homesteads, destroying crops and rustling cattle – beef he later sold, running them with his own brand. Finding a rough-and-ready Mexican crew was not difficult. The border country was, as was most of Mexico, wallowing in poverty and rife with unrest, as the undemocratic and corrupt rule of President Portifio Diaz offered little reward to the people for their labour or their loyalty. They, like the Yaqui, accepted Vagg's almighty US dollar happily. The border was but a river and their guns served him well, as many of the frustrated and frightened homesteaders loaded their waggons and whatever belongings were transportable and headed back to the north, as far from the border as possible. Of course, supplying guns to the renegade and restless Mescalero Apaches helped fan the flames.

Vagg paid what he considered to be a fair price for any land purchased, although that was a basic price without any consideration of the hard, backbreaking work the small ranchers or homesteaders had put into their small and often insignificant holdings. But a lot of little, unimportant things joined together made one big thing, and most of the land now in his possession was in line with the route proposed by the government, should the railway move that way; he was given to understand it would. There were still a few stubborn men who refused to sell, but in due course he would slowly persuade them to see the error of their ways.

He tucked the thick, woven Indian blanket around him as the chill of the damp air drifted up from the river and invaded his frail bones. He was lonely, he was still suffering a little from his last chew of Peyote, and Margaret was in San Antonio visiting friends and gathering valuable information. He needed a drinking companion. He picked up a small brass bell that sat by his empty glass and dirty supper plate and gently rang it. Within seconds, Miguel, his Mexican servant, appeared and refilled the wine glass silently – something he was allowed to do only when Frank Vagg was dining alone – and removed the empty plate, asking, 'Is there anything else, *señor*?'

'A fresh cigar, Miguel, and find Mr Temple. Bring another glass and fetch him here for me.' His voice was softly tinged with a southern accent adopted from his young years spent in Virginia.

The servant returned moments later, poured a fresh glass of wine and said, 'Mr Temple is on his way over, *señor*. He will be here *en un momento*.'

Vagg nodded and rolled the cigar between his finger and thumb before lighting it with a waxed taper fired by the oil-fuelled table lamp.

'You wanted me, Mr Vagg?'

Jack Temple was a tall man, dressed from head to toe in black. He looked ageless, his years difficult to discern. Vagg had always assumed him to be around sixty years old, but it was hard to tell. The man's hair was still full and dark with just a touch of grey at the temples. His face was very much wrinkle-free and clean-shaven but for the full drooping moustache, and his voice was like Vagg's: distinctly southern and only a little above a whisper. Vagg had never known the man to raise it more. He wore a patch over his right eye and the jet-black left eye twinkled in the flickering light of the lamp. He was one of the only two men he really trusted and did trust daily with his well-being. Temple watched his back and kept him company on long evenings when Margaret was away in San Antonio, which was often. The only other man of any real intellect on the payroll was the albino, Val Lefranc, and Lefranc's main concern was for the twenty-four hour safety of Margaret Vagg. In fact, he fulfilled exactly the same function for her as Temple did for him. The pale-eyed, white-skinned man with his mane of long white hair was a lean one; rail thin, but like the rattler that some called him, he could pull his head back and be at an assailant's throat in a heartbeat. With his strong hands, a knife or a gun, Lefranc was a man to walk around.

'Sit down, Jack. Take the weight off and have a glass of wine. Help yourself to a cigar if would like one.'

Temple declined the smoke, taking out the makings from his vest pocket and preferring to roll his own.

'How's Jimmy?' Vagg asked quietly.

'I've never seen an angrier man in my life, but he will be OK.'

'Good. His hearing affected?'

'Apart from a temporary ringing, I do not believe so. The shooter was good and only took off the fleshy part of the ear.'

'This shooter, Jack, we know anything about him?'

'No, sir. Seems Jimmy picked on the man and chose the wrong man to pick on. It happens.'

'Willy Jones brought him home. Says the man calls himself the Peaceful River Kid. You ever heard of him?'

Temple smiled, 'No, sir, and I am not sure he calls himself by that name, either. It seems he signed the hotel register as Louis Bassett of Wichita, and Kansas is some long ways away from the Peaceful River.'

'Where did it come from then?'

'It would appear our sheriff has a flier on such an outlaw with a similar appearance, but as with any sobriquet. . . . You know how these things are, how they grow.'

'Sometimes I do and sometimes I don't, but he may need watching if he is not riding through.'

'My feeling is he is just a drifter, possibly on the dodge and hoping to lose himself along the border like so many others, but I can have a word with him if you like.' The inference was not lost on Vagg, but he chose to ignore it.

'Keep your ear to the ground, Jack, but hold off for the moment. I don't want to call attention to us at this precise moment, and please pass that on to the men. I don't want any more gunplay. Worst comes to the worst, I'll send Monroe to have a word with him. He must be quite handy with a Colt, though, to take down Jimmy with such ease as to place a round through his fucking ear.'

Vagg was not usually given to profanity and Temple noticed the concern in the elderly man's tone.

'Will there be anything else, sir?'

Vagg was quiet for a long moment, rolling the cigar between thumb and forefinger as he blew tiny smoke rings out into the still air. 'No, not really, Jack. You handle the business side and my security very well, but I look around and I think we need to bring in a man to run the roughnecks. The Mex we hire, they seem to sit around most of the day doing very little.'

'You did not hire them as cattlemen, sir.'

'True, but you get the feeling things are a little lax around here. It needs considering. . . . Maybe this drifter would be interested in a job; he seems to know how to handle trouble. Who knows, eh, Jack, who knows?'

'Could be, Mr Vagg.'

'I'll study on it some and let you know. Margaret will be home shortly. We'll see what she has learned from that loose-tongued banker she flirts with.'

'And in the meantime. . . ?'

'Sit awhile, will you, Jack? Finish your wine. Have another if you have a mind to, and pass the word: I want no repercussions from last evening.' Then, adding as an afterthought, 'You might also mention I heard a raven today, so one must be close by. Tell them I've upped the bounty by four bits.'

Temple nodded, finished his drink, then poured another and sat quietly beside Vagg long into the cool evening.

CHAPTER EIGHT

HENRIETTA LARSSON

The rain came late into the evening and cooled the unpredictably warm air enough for me to strip to the waist, lie back on the hard mattress, turn down the oil lamp and enjoy the scent of the wet night as it drifted in through the open window. South Texas: one evening you are freezing and the next baking. I was listening to the rhythm of the falling rain beating on the upper half-closed window glass, relaxing. Deciding to stay indoors, I was pulling off a boot, but the gentle tap on my door was an unwanted intrusion. I got up from the bed with a groan, my back still a little stiff from the long Overland stage's bone-shaking ride. I pulled my hideaway .45 Derringer from my discarded boot and opened the door onto the dimly lit hall.

She was a tall, lean, indiscernible shadow against the flickering lamp. She looked down at the pistol and then straight back to me. 'Are you pleased to see me or what?'

I sensed lightness in her tone and felt a little foolish standing there with one boot on and gun in my hand. 'Henri Larsson, I presume,' was all I could think of to say.

'My, you really are a detective aren't you, Kid?'

It wasn't really a question, so I ignored it.

'Kid?' I said, stepping back and widening the opening so that she could get inside without brushing against me.

'You are the infamous Peaceful River Kid, are you not?'

She turned to face me as I closed the door and went to the bedside to turn up the lamp a little. A tad taller than me, straight and slim without a loss of shape. Dark hair, raven black it looked to be. Her face, at least in the half-light, appeared to be slightly masculine with a firm chin, a gentle mouth and laughing eyes – laughing at me, I thought. I kicked off my remaining boot, set the gun on the table and drew the curtains before returning my attention to her directly. 'There is no such person; it's a made-up name I found to be useful a couple of times, and I would prefer you did not make reference to it again.'

'Oh, a rose by any other name would smell as sweet?'

'*Romeo and Juliet*,' I said, 'and not very original.'

'I heard you were well read. You always come to the door half-dressed and with your pistol in your hand?'

I felt that she was laughing at me, but it did not seem to matter; I have been laughed at before. I dug a clean and very rumpled faded red shirt out of my warbag and put it on. Her eyes seemed to follow my every move. Unnerving.

'That tattoo on your shoulder, is that a crow?' Then, answering her own question, 'Why a crow?'

'It's not a crow; it's a raven. Bigger than a crow, meaner, smarter.'

'Tattoos are not that common out here.'

'And neither are ravens, apparently.'

'Our man Frank Vagg has a bounty on them.'

'You've seen a lot of half-naked tattooed men?' I asked, changing the subject.

'Not too many, but a few when I worked at a hospital in San Antonio before I joined the Pinkertons. Just interested; does it represent anything?'

'Should it?'

'Sometimes they are the result of an evening of drunken madness, sometimes just for decoration and other times for very personal reasons. I went out with a Texas Ranger one time who had a diamondback tattooed on his shoulder. Turned out he was a bit of a snake also. Are you a raven, a dark bird?'

I ignored her and poured myself a whiskey. 'Would you care for one?'

'Do you have a clean glass?'

We sat there in silence for a few moments, she in the

room's single chair and me back on the bed, propped up on the pillow jammed against the headboard. The only sound apart from our breathing was the patter of the rain as it gathered pace, backed by a rising southerly wind.

'Did you know Kathleen Riley?' I asked, wanting to get that subject out of the way, lest it hover.

'Briefly. I also know how she died. I also know that you could not have done anything about it. Line of duty: a risk we all take.'

'You carry a piece?'

'It's against company policy.'

It wasn't an answer but I let it slide. 'Mind if I smoke?'

She shook her head and sipped her whiskey. 'I've been here a week now. Nothing to say really that would help you. At least, nothing that you would not have discovered for yourself out on the street. I got myself a job at the Overland stage office, working the mail mostly, and selling tickets, keeping the place tidy . . . not much else to do around here for a girl who can't sing, can't dance and would not know one good poker hand from another.' She smiled. 'Three jobs I was offered at the Red Diamond Saloon. I have now been offered a part-time position at the land office; that may be a fatter cow to milk. Should the need ever arise, I can also read and work the telegraph, but I have not let that be known.'

I nodded and waited.

'Vagg has a raggle-taggle bunch of men on his

payroll; mostly they drink and hurrah south of the line. Billy Bob is a cautious man, but he will only let them go so far before he hangs up his fishing rod and does his day job of keeping law and order. He seems to have the full support of Vagg where law in this part of town is concerned.'

'He is a strange man, sure enough. He braced me about the flier that Beaufort sent out but let it slide; not out of fear but seemingly a lack of interest.'

'Vagg's ramrod is Jimmy Olds, but you have already met him, I understand.'

'I tried to talk him out of a fight but he would not listen.'

'And now I am told he does not hear so good anymore.' She smiled. 'He also has two other men working for him who sound to be of a much higher calibre.'

'Have you met them?'

'No, but I do know their names: Jack Temple and an albino by the name Val Lefranc.'

'Jack Temple? You are sure that is his name?'

'That's what I am told. Why, do you know him? He is a one-eyed man; wears an eye patch, apparently. There seems to be a bit of confusion as to which eye it covers.'

I did not answer right away, thinking on it. Then I simply nodded.

'He is Vagg's personal bodyguard and Lefranc serves the same purpose for his sister. I understand they are away at present, possibly in San Antonio, but

Temple is on the ranch and never comes into town unless it is to accompany Vagg.'

'Good, all useful intelligence,' I said. 'Another drink?'

'No, thank you.' She got to her feet and walked over to the bed. 'My room is just down the hall. You need anything – or for me to contact head office – just slip a note under the door. If I need anything, I will do the same. Goodnight, Kid, and thanks for the drink.'

She was out through the door before I had the chance to object, and I think I heard her chuckle as she closed it behind her.

CHAPTER NINE

HECTOR MONROE

The man was big, as big a man as they come: high, wide and ugly. I figured he could eat me for a light breakfast if he wanted to; he looked hungry and I felt very tired. I am not used to a long day in the saddle: my backside was tender, my inappropriate town suit draped in dust, my shirt wet with sweat, and I needed a drink, a bath and a shave in that order. I had spent the day exploring the flat grassy landscape to the north of town. Other than a few deserted homesteads, two burned out, and abandoned crops, I had found little of interest. As soon as I saw the big man, I knew those priorities would mean very little to him. I bellied up to the bar, ordered a beer without a head and we studied each other in the long mirror. As we studied on each other, the small crowd of late afternoon drinkers waited patiently for whatever was going to happen. I guessed they knew who the big man was.

He spoke to my reflection in the mirror. 'You the man shot the ear off my friend, Jimmy the Deuce?'

I should have known Jimmy would have a friend.

'Is that a question or a statement of fact?' I said to his reflection.

'Either will do if you be he.'

His voice was fairly high pitched and did not sound to be coming from such a big fellow. He was dressed in faded dungarees with a corncob pipe stem jutting out of the bib. He was not wearing a sidearm and, as far as I could tell, there were no lumps or bumps in the overalls that suggested a knife or hidden weapon. He was clean-shaven and shorthaired, with a benign open face that looked as if it had been moulded from wet clay by a none-too-skilful sculptor. He had a large cauliflower ear and his nose looked like it had been reshaped a time or two, but the eyes were dark and alive, and there was the hint of a smile on his fat lips. *The expectations of a great pleasure yet to come?* I wondered.

'Who sent you?' I asked quietly. 'Is there an endless supply of folk around here who do not like me? I'm an OK fellow if you get to know me.'

'No one sent me. I came because you hurt my friend, is all, and I figure to give you back some of the same.'

So, there it was, out in the open with no subterfuge. He was there to kick my ass and he, and I suspect the spectators, had little doubt that was what was going to happen. Seems I was the source of some unusual entertainment since my arrival in San Pedro. First there had been a gunman who wanted to shoot me dead, and now a hungry giant of a man who seemed intent on eating me. I looked around but there was no sign of Billy Bob Hunt, so I figured he had gone fishing again.

I am no fist-fighter; I am too slight by far and I rarely, if ever, put myself in a position where pure physical violence is the only possible outcome. I have no wish to have my nose broken or my teeth kicked out. Probably more to the point, given my profession, I could not afford to damage my hands – especially not my right hand. My face is already much too lived in, and my gun hand keeps me alive.

He turned to face me. 'You are such a little man. I was told you was a big old boy.'

'A little rattler can kill you as dead as a big one,' I said. 'Might take a little longer, but dead is dead and the snake couldn't give a damn.'

'I ain't packing. You can't shoot an unarmed man down, not even in this burg.'

'Who says I can't?' I offered with what I hoped was a cold smile.

'Feisty little bastard, ain't you just? Best get running though, I'll give you that chance. You run hard and fast and me and Jimmy will call it quits. How does that sound? That, or I'll stomp the living daylights out of you.'

'Never ran away from any man in my life, sir, and I do not intend to start today.' Before the last word was out of my mouth, I was running straight at him and charging the cannon. He was as much surprised as the spectators. When I was a couple of feet from him I lashed out with my pointed boot, driving the toe hard and deep into his crotch. It must have hurt like hell. His eyes crossed and his knees banged together, and he let out one great moan and sank to the floor. I stepped closer, drew my Colt and smacked him across the temple. It took two taps to make him keel over, blood running down his deathly white face.

It was over. It would be a while before he could walk upright and longer before he would be inclined to sit a saddle. I holstered my piece and knelt beside him, nodding to the open-mouthed bartender. 'Bring me a brandy, a large one.'

I took the glass from the man's shaking hand and held it to the lips of the big man. 'Drink this down, breath deep, think of something nice and hold those *cojones* tight, my friend, before they drop off. Get some ice on them as soon as possible. They will be sore for a while, but no permanent damage.'

He stared up at me and nodded. I ordered and gave him another brandy, and helped him to his feet and supported his immense weight to an empty table. 'You got a friend here? I mean a real friend.'

He nodded and whispered a name.

I looked around the room and recognised the little man who had been in company with Jimmy Olds. I called him over. 'Your name Willy Jones?' I asked.

'Yes, sir.'

'Well, Willy Jones, seems you don't have too much

luck with the company you keep. I suggest you get a buckboard and you take this big fellow back to whichever hell cave he came from, and tell whoever sent him that little rattlers bite hard.'

As I helped get the big man laid out as comfortable as possible on the flat bed of the buckboard, he looked up at me, the watering eyes still pain-filled. 'I won't forget this, Mister,' and he squeezed my hand, almost gently I think. It reassured me that he meant the words in the best possible way and that they were in no way intended as a threat.

Suddenly, Billy Bob Hunt was at my shoulder. 'You surely do surprise a fellow, Mr Bassett. I have never seen anyone put Heck Monroe on his back before and never expected to.'

'You have not seen the worst of me, Billy Bob. You should see me when I am really angry.'

I left him to think that over and made my way over to Ben's barbershop for a shave, and then to the hotel for a hot bath. As I crossed the street, I saw Henri Larsson watching from the open door of the Overland stage office. She was smiling but did not wave.

CHAPTER TEN

THE ONE-EYED MAN

The day following my encounter with Heck Monroe, I bought a length of fishing line, some hooks, a bobber and a sinker. Following a quick visit to the sheriff's office, I set out to the clearwater stream he was so fond of visiting on stormy days, when to stay in town would have threatened his health some. Billy Bob was delighted to draw me a little map showing the location of Springwater Creek and the whereabouts of the best deep holes nearest to the town. He sounded genuinely regretful that he could not join me, but taxes were due and it was a profitable part of his job as county sheriff to collect them.

By noon I had a couple of brace, four fair-sized crappies strung out on a line in the shallows, awaiting my appetite to reach a pitch where I could get enough enthusiasm together to build a small campfire and cook a pair of them. I was settled on a soft grass patch with the Morgan hobbled a few yards from me, my hat over my eyes, and half covered by the newspaper I had borrowed from the lobby of the Wayfarer's Hotel.

'You look pretty peaceful, Kid. I guess the name stuck. You should be more careful, though; you are not the most popular man in Riverton County.' The voice was almost a whisper.

I looked up at the one-eyed man, and moved the newspaper from where it covered my hand and revealed the Colt that was levelled at his belly. 'I had you spotted ten minutes ago, old man, when you showed your head above that rise beyond the willows.'

He laughed. 'You can put that piece away. Were I really dogging you, my hat would not have been above that rise, Kid.'

'The Peaceful River Kid does not exist. How many times do I have to tell people?'

Jack Temple squatted down beside me and took the makings from his shirt pocket, rolled a cigarette and tossed me the sack of Durham. 'You caught anything?'

'A couple of brace of crappies. I was just thinking about building a fire under two them when I saw your big hat out there. What the hell are you doing this far south?'

'I might ask you the same question.'

We lit our smokes from the same match and I stared into his right pale blue eye. 'If my memory serves me correctly – and it usually does – last time I saw you, that patch was on your right eye and the left eye was black. Today it's on the left and your right eye is pale blue.'

'I like to keep folk guessing.'

'It is called heterochromia,' I said, enjoying the taste of the smoke.

'Not many people know that,' Temple said.

'I am well-read,' I said.

'Louis Bassett of Wichita, Kansas, last time I saw you, if my memory serves me correctly, you were holding a busted flush and had rankled the hell out of three men enough for them to kill you. You still trying to fill inside straights?'

'When I get the chance; it's a bad habit. I have more than most.'

'I thought you were long dead. You must keep your head down.'

'Mostly along the east coast, Louisiana, New Orleans, the river boats, boom towns wherever there is loose money to be found. Worked cattle for a while, but my backside complained.'

Lying comes easily to me; maybe I should have been a politician.

'You a rich man now, Kid?'

'At this very moment, dirt poor, but I'm going to try my luck below the border; seems there is some federal paper out on me this side of the river.'

'So I have heard. You also seem to have been a busy man here: shot the ear off one of my employer's top hands, kicked the crap out of another.'

'Your employer Frank Vagg, by any chance?'

'By every chance.'

'Like I said, I have a lot of unpleasant habits and getting shot or beaten to death are not among them. And stop calling me Kid; I'm just coming to terms with being an old man.'

'OK, Mr Bassett, I may have a proposition for you.' He put a big emphasis on the word 'Mr'.

'And that would be. . . ?'

'My employer is looking for a man who can handle men, knows cattle and isn't afraid to get his hands a little dirty, if you know what I mean.'

'I'm not sure that I do.'

'Yes, you do. Anyway, think it over and let me know. Come out to the Circle and meet the old man. He's pretty impressed by the way you handled two of his best men.'

'This Mr Vagg . . . he ever come to town? I mean, this side of the river?'

'Once a week, maybe.'

'Well, you tell him next time he comes to come see me. I'm staying at the Wayfarer's and do not fancy a long ride for what might turn out to be a waste of both our times.'

Temple stubbed his cigarette out on a rock and said, 'You going to eat both of those crappies, Mr Bassett? If not, we can share them, and the bottle I have in my saddle-bag.'

'Call me Lou,' I said, 'and get the bottle while I get a fire under them fish.'

Dark thunderheads were gathering over the grey granite cliffs, and there was a defined smell of rain on the breeze that drifted down from the rocky escarpments to the far west of San Pedro. It would be a wet night.

CHAPTER ELEVEN

PASTEBOARDS CANNOT SHOOT

Later that evening, washed up and the dust brushed from my town suit, I slipped a note under Henri Larsson's door asking her to come to my room if convenient. It was, and ten minutes later I answered her brief knock on my door.

'Both of your boots on, fully clothed and no pistol: oh my, Kid, you have come a long way.'

She was smiling and I simply rolled my eyes, turned down the lamp a little and closed the door behind her. There was something about her I liked: not just her flashing eyes, her dark hair or her soft voice. Something more than that: there was a whole person there, hidden behind a façade of lightness. It was as if, for some strange reason, she was a little uncertain of herself in my company. Not in any way in awe of me but of my reputation that, within the agency and without exaggeration, was something I was not overly proud of. I was considered by some to be a loose cannon, which on occasions was of use to them, and on others something of an embarrassment. This feeling did not extend to Agent in Charge Joshua Beaufort or young Benbow, and to others I had worked with, but to newly appointed agents. I guess old tales stuck, and my last case had ended in bloodshed and disaster with little to show for it other than the death of a fellow agent. In the larger scheme of things, it was a success. However, it was a case closed, and with the approval and appreciation of the US Government and the attorney general. An acceptable result to the officers, maybe, but not necessarily to the troops – the field agents who risk their lives daily in the pursuit of justice. The circumstances of Kathleen Riley's death would always walk in my shadow within the agency. These things I understand, but they nevertheless trouble and confuse me.

'Sit down, make yourself comfortable, drink, smoke, sing and dance if you want, but for heaven's sake, stop calling me Kid. I'm damn near old enough to be your father.' I turned down the lamp a little more, set two glasses on the small table and poured us a couple of drinks.

'Does it really bother you that much?' She had a lovely voice, a mere hint of an accent, and her words were not wrapped in a smile this time as they usually were.

Strangely enough, I felt it to be a genuine question.

'Yes, more so from you than anyone.'

'Then I will cease henceforth, sir, and I am sorry if I offended you.'

'Damn it,' I said, 'you haven't offended me, it's just, it's just, it's. . . .' I was lost for words, and that was unusual for me.

She walked over to me and held out her right hand. 'Agent Larsson reporting for duty, Lucas. The smile was back but it was a serious kind of a smile; almost a sad smile.

I took her hand and held it a little longer than necessary, released it, threw my best winning smile at her, passed her a glass and tapped it with mine. 'Looking forward to working with you, Agent Larsson.'

'Likewise. Now to the business in hand.'

I stared out of the closed window, listening to her soft voice as she told of her discoveries working both in the post office and her short stint in the Land Registry office. Outside the promised rain arrived, backed by a strong wind and sheet lightning that lit up the rocky background to the east side of Main Street. Two men rode in, splashing through the puddles formed on the hardbacked soil, their yellow slickers glistening in the reflected afterglow of the lightning. They rode straight into the open doors of the livery and, moments later, ran out and headed for the Red Diamond. I wondered why they bothered to run; they must have already been soaked through to the skin.

'Nothing much to report from the post office: some mail from San Antonio for Vagg and a couple of empty

Wells Fargo boxes for the Merchant Bank.' She sipped her drink and I refilled my glass. 'Interesting find in the land office, though. Seems Vagg has been buying up a lot of land to the east of the town but avoided any from the west. Seems he prefers the flat land to the rocky ground of the west. Also of interest to you is that he hasn't filed on much of it yet at the county seat in Riverton, but his sister has.'

'Perhaps he is just acquisitive, one of those ranchers who maybe cannot stand neighbours, but it is worth noting and maybe I can use it. Find an easterly property nearer to town that hasn't been homestead proved; maybe he would like me as a neighbour. Better yet, find me one that she hasn't yet filed. Stir them up a little.'

'You find anything on your ride out?'

'Nothing much to say on that, other than he is coming to town shortly and may be offering me a job as a trouble-shooter on the Circle V.'

'Where did you hear that?'

'Long story. I will let you know if it actually happens.'

That answer did not exactly please her.

We talked long into the evening, and I was conscious that I had missed supper and the alcohol was having some effect on my thinking.

'Do you not like working with me, Lucas, or is it just because I am a woman?'

Her words, after one long silence, caught me unawares.

I thought about her question long and hard. It deserved a thoughtful answer if I could find one. 'No, I am happy enough to work with you, but I have not fared well with partners over the years. Several of them have ended up dead; even my wife was killed because of me. I seem to be a magnet for bullets.'

She thought about that while I refilled our glasses. 'Life is just one big tragedy for all of us. We are all born to die, some sooner than others; it cannot be avoided.'

'To some extent it can be,' I said. 'You have a bad hand, you throw it in; you walk away, never draw to an inside straight . . . that way you can shorten the odds and maybe stay in the game a little longer.'

'Why play the game if you cannot afford to take a chance? It is your choice, as it is the choice of others who wish to be near you. I could walk away tomorrow if I was worried about your behaviour. Beaufort would support me in that.'

'It is not that simple,' I said. 'Sometimes you ride your luck. You stay in a game a hand too long and walk away with nothing or, in some cases, you don't walk away at all.'

The sheet lightning bounced back around the town, lighting up the room momentarily, and I could see her staring at me, thinking I knew not what. 'Like I said, it is a choice. I signed on for this,' she said eventually.

I shook my head and chewed the inside of my lower lip, something I was apt to do when thinking too deeply. 'So, you believe, like Shakespeare, that all the world's a stage, that we are merely players and our entrances and exits are preordained?'

She got to her feet and faced me across the room, her figure framed in lightning: a vision, a disturbing vision.

'You know something, Lucas Santana? You read too much.' Then the smile. 'That may be a better thing to believe in than that your exit is realised through the mere turn of a Bicycle playing card.'

'A pasteboard cannot shoot.'

'True, but the man turning that card for you can. Goodnight, Lucas.'

She brushed past me, touched my arm gently, opened the door and was gone. I stood by the window for a long time, watching the night. Presently the two riders, still in their slickers and somewhat unsteady on their feet, walked into the stable and emerged five minutes later, walking their mounts carefully on Main Street, and headed south.

CHAPTER TWELVE

THE RAVENS

The following morning, more suitably dressed in faded Levi's and wearing an equally faded denim shirt, I consulted the rough map Agent Henri Larsson had produced for me. I set out to explore the countryside to the west of San Pedro.

The immediate terrain to both the east and west of San Pedro was much the same: rocky backdrops, high grey bluffs dropping down to green pasture and green wooded land. That green giving way to brown marshy, sandy soil leading to the actual river, which was running low, and crossable without getting a boot full of water. The main difference was that to the east the land flattened out quite quickly, whereas to the west the escarpment got higher and the terrain less attractive to horse or rider. It would take me more than one day to cover both and I thought to get the harder ride over and done with would better suit by backside.

The countryside was littered with run-down and abandoned dwellings, homesteads mostly, with a sprinkling of small two by four ranches. The homesteads were the saddest. Some had been deserted in a hurry, leaving behind the too-heavy-to-tote trappings of what once was family life: a piano, a rocking chair, a table and a child's toys, a rag doll in a play crib, books and clothes. Barns with harness and tools still where they were last stored, and maybe used. In the back of one there were two graves, their markers indicating that they were the last resting places of two children left behind, with no one to tend their graves. I spent a few minutes clearing the tumbleweed and the long grass from them and straightening and reseating their markers. John and Bridget Faulkner, both ten years old. Twins, maybe. I wondered where their parents were and if they were still alive, or if, like their children, they were buried beneath the fertile land that bounded this area of the Rio Grande valley.

I saw few signs of wildlife and a total absence of ravens, birds that were usually so prolific in those rocky parts of the Texas border country. The smell of Mexican food drifted across the wide river, and with it the occasional sound of music and once the sound of rifle fire. I turned back northwest after watering the hired Morgan in the big river; he was a sure-footed animal and did not seem to object to the rough terrain. Avoiding the Rio, telling myself it was not a good day to visit Mexico, I headed toward what my map told me was the land owned and occupied by the mysterious Frank Vagg. The stink of death and decay reached me as I entered a small stand of cottonwoods. It was a stench the wildflowers that bloomed in abundance in their shelter could not hide. The Morgan snorted its displeasure but I pushed him on, wanting to be clear of it myself. Passing a large cottonwood, the source of the stink became clear. It also answered my question of the missing ravens: they were all there, a long line of wire stretched from tall tree to tall tree and dressed in dead birds. Several hundred ravens in various stages of decay draped on what trappers called the Vermin Pole. Beneath the hanging birds were the remains of several hundred more; birds that had once dressed the wire and had now fallen to become part of the earth from which they came. It was a pitiful and disgusting sight, and for a moment I felt an overwhelming anger – rage, really – that quickly dissipated as I considered my options of venting that rage and finding nothing there. It was done.

I hobbled the Morgan in the grassy shade of a small stand of Ponderosa pine and continued on foot after changing into a pair moccasins purchased from the general store that morning. Pointy-toed, high-heeled riding boots are not compatible to walking over rough ground. After a couple of hours wandering I had seen a lot more than I expected. Cattle roamed loose everywhere, many of them unbranded. Small groups of men gathered in the shade playing cards or sleeping, some with a small campfire burning under a blackened coffee pot. They were, by and large, a mixed bunch of men, neither cowboys nor gunmen: a raggletaggle bunch of individuals from both sides of the borderline, men in range clothes and all well armed. They seemed at a loss as to how best to spend their time. I was briefly tempted to wander down and join one group in the hope of a hot coffee, but slipped through the trees behind them and moved on to where I thought I had heard the distressed cry of a raven.

First, I found the man's horse tied off to a large fallen branch. I paused and listened again for the forlorn sound of the bird. Ravens have many voices and this one was obviously distressed. I picked my way quietly through the brush until I detected the heavy smell of pipe tobacco on the clear air.

He was dressed much as the men I had seen, partially hidden behind a brush screen, sitting cross-legged, a rifle across his lap and a corncob pipe jutting from his bearded face. A little to his left and below, close by to a puddle of the overnight rainwater, he had staked out a juvenile raven as, I supposed, bait for other birds. Its leg was tied by a leather thong to a wooden stake wedged firmly into a cleft in the hard rock. One wing draped the ground, but it seems it had long ago given up the fight. A mewing sound was heard, its head bent toward the water, which was just out of reach.

The man did not hear my approach and I jammed

my Colt hard into the hollow of his neck and cocked it. He froze and the smoking pipe dropped from his mouth.

He started to turn and I jabbed the Colt in harder. 'Not a word,' I said quietly. 'Not even a whisper.' I pulled back the gun and slapped him very hard alongside the head with the steel barrel, stepping clear as he rolled back toward me, dead to the world.

I carefully picked up the young raven, familiar with the bird as I had a tame one as a kid. For a long time it had been my only companion, the brightest of birds. This one settled in my hands after I had cut his restraint with my folding knife, and I carried him to the edge of the small pool. He drank, filling his beak and holding his head back as he swallowed the cool water, but made no attempt to fly away. His wing settled back to its normal position and he sat on my hat for an hour or so, watching carefully as I tied the hands of his captor and attached his booted feet to the peg vacated by the raven. Seemingly satisfied with my actions, he made a squawking noise, whistled, and hobbled to the edge of the clearing. He looked back just the once before launching himself down the escarpment, flying too close to the ground for a while before gaining lift and soaring upwards and over the rocky cliff and lost to my sight.

'What the hell . . .' the man said, shaking his head as he emerged from the darkness of his unexpected sleep and finding himself tethered as had been his Judas bird. 'Cut me loose, damn it.'

81

'You have two chances, Mister. Maybe your friends will find you, or you may free yourself; the restraints are not that firm. Either way, I will look back this way in a couple of days and if you are still here and a big cat hasn't found you, I will free you or bury you.'

'I get out of this, I will find and kill you. You can't ride far and fast enough.'

'The ramblings of a fool,' I said, removing his neckerchief and using it as a gag, 'and best to go unheard.' I left him there with those few words of wisdom, wondering what he made of them and why I had not told Henri Larsson about the inspiration for my tattoo.

CHAPTER THIRTEEN

MARGARET VAGG

Frank Vagg was an impatient man. Several of his life-shaping decisions on the long journey from the green pastures of Virginia to the dusty border town of San Pedro had been hasty and spur-of-the-moment affairs. Some had worked out while others had not, but he had learned one valuable lesson, and that was not to press his sister. Margaret Vagg had arrived home that morning. The liveryman's surrey had brought her, Lefranc and her moderate luggage back out to the Circle V. She was dusty and irritable, and insisted on a hot bath and a change of clothes before reporting in full to her brother. Vagg settled on the porch and chewed on a cheroot, fighting the urge that boiled within him to know of her news from San Antonio.

Margaret Vagg was, like her older brother, slight of stature but not to such a degree as to be unattractive to men. An inch or so taller than Vagg, with auburn hair, a pale, high-cheekbone face and piercing blue eyes that could at one and the same time attract the attention of a man and warn him that it was not an open invitation to flirt; that was left to her full red lipped mouth. Those lips, if the eyes agreed, could welcome a kiss, but if they did not then the curl of the upper lip could destroy him in an instant. Margaret Vagg was very aware of these facts and used them to profound effect while dining and dancing in San Antonio at the expense of the businessmen who sought her out, not only for her own charms, but for the fact that any dealings with Frank Vagg could sometimes lead to a healthy profit.

Vagg looked up, dogged his cheroot and got to his feet, giving her a gentle hug and a kiss on each cheek as she reached him and sat herself beside him. 'Drink, Marge, dear?' he asked.

She hated being called Marge, but it was his little intimacy and she bore it, albeit somewhat grudgingly. 'I have asked Miguel to bring us a bottle of chilled white wine and two glasses,' she said quietly, a deep, pleasant voice that, given the occasion, could render a good tune.

'How was San Antonio? Worthwhile, I hope?'

'That depends, brother mine.'

'On what?'

'On how we move forward from here.' She took a

84

small leather-bound book and sheaf of papers from her purse and set them in front of him.

Vagg gave them a cursory inspection and pushed them to one side. He waited knowing she would condense their content in a few clear and concise sentences if she so wished.

Miguel, the manservant, brought a silver tray, a jug of ice, a bottle and two long stemmed wine glasses. He uncorked the bottle as was his duty but knew better than to pour the wine. That, as always, was the master's task.

They sat there in the early afternoon sunshine, sipping their wine and making small talk about the ranch until, much to Vagg's relief, she told him of her visit to the halls of power in uptown San Antonio.

'Things are not as they were when I last visited. There are nervous men everywhere. Talk is that the railroad could go either way, and only one of them is our way.' She reached for the box of cheroots on the table and Vagg leaned forward and fired it for her. She inhaled deeply and, tipping her head back, blew the smoke into the air above them before stubbing the smoke out in the ashtray provided earlier by Miguel. 'Filthy habit,' she said. 'Tobacco on the breath of a man is not pleasant, so I would guess it to be doubly unpleasant to a man on the breath of a woman.'

'And the other?' Vagg asked, ignoring her thoughts on tobacco as he had so many times before.

'Diablo is on, all good there; we will receive more

information and details on that in the next two weeks, but I have no doubt that is ours for the taking.'

Vagg could not hide his delight and whooped, laughed and drained his glass. 'If the railroad comes here then we will make a killing, enough at least to leave this godforsaken place and return to a comfortable enough civilisation. Great, but if Diablo pays off then we will be walking in tall cotton for the rest of our lives; now that is something to look forward to.'

'How have things been here, Frank? I saw Jimmy Olds skulking out by the barn with a large bandage on the side of his head and Heck Monroe sitting on the bunkhouse stoop, looking to be the saddest man I ever did see. He hardly acknowledged my passing; so unlike him.'

'The men are restless, bored maybe. Jimmy took it upon himself to roust a stranger in town and said stranger shot his ear off. I sent Monroe into town to see to this *hombre* and he put poor old Heck on his back with a kick to that region on a man's body that is most vulnerable.'

'He kicked him in the *cojones*? Poor old Heck, he won't be riding for a spell then.'

Vagg winced; there was a certain vulgarity about his sister of which he did not approve, but which he accepted, knowing it was one of the so-called virtues that endeared her to the rich and the powerful men of San Antonio. She could, at one and the same time, be one of the boys or one of the girls, depending upon her own needs. 'I guess not,' was all he could think to say.

'What do you intend to do about the men here? We cannot afford to draw any attention to this place; at least not until we have finished with it.'

'That's exactly what I told Temple.'

'And what did good old Jack say. . . ?

Vagg ignored the sarcasm in her tone, knowing full well that his sister did not approve of his reliance on the bodyguard. 'I suggested and he agreed that we hire this stranger, have him on the inside of the house pissing out rather than on the outside pissing in, so to speak.'

'Delicately put as usual, Frank.'

He dismissed her remark with a thin-shouldered shrug. 'I am just saying, is all.'

'Who is he? What is he? Would he take the job?' she said.

'Billy Bob says there is a federal warrant on the man from sometime back, and Jack says he knew him a long time ago in Wichita. Got in a bit of a hole there, according to Jack. Says he's called the Peaceful River Kid but no one other than Jack seems to have heard of him. Whatever, I am in town day after tomorrow so Jack will introduce us. We'll see how it goes.'

'I'm coming with you: I have to see the man fast enough to outshoot Jimmy the Deuce and hard enough to beat up on Hector Monroe. He must be some kind of a man; the kind of a man I would like to meet.'

Vagg did not like the licentious chuckle that followed her words, but knew only too well that it would be useless to object to her company.

CHAPTER FOURTEEN

INVITATION WITH A SHOTGUN

It was little Willy Jones, the unfortunate companion of both Jimmy the Deuce and Big Heck Monroe, who braced me somewhat nervously at the bar of the Red Diamond. I looked up from my newspaper, dropped my reading glasses an inch or two and stared down at him over the metal topped frames. He cleared his throat several times but was having trouble with the words.

'Come on, Willy, have you brought another little friend for me to fool around with? Been kind of a slow day?'

'Mr Vagg would like you to join him over at the

Drover's Club for a private dinner and drink, sir.' Jones stuttered out the words.

'I already ate,' I said.

'Perhaps, Mr Bassett, just for the drink then?'

'He told you to say that?'

'Yes, sir: he said if it were too late for dinner, would you please join him for a nightcap? Those were his exact words.'

I could not help feeling sorry for the little man; he had seen me shoot his friend's ear off and then floor another buddy with a crotch kick. He looked at me like he was a pack rat face-to-face with a sidewinder and with nowhere run. 'Look, Jonesy, you tell your boss that if he wants to talk to me then I am in the Red Diamond. I would be happy to share a nightcap with him. You tell him I am kind of comfortable here right now.' I turned back to my paper and watched him in the long bar mirror as he crossed the room and walked out into the flickering darkness.

An hour later, after a pleasant jaw with Ben the barber I shared a drink quietly with Mort Cullis the undertaker, a friendly but sombre-looking man befitting of his trade. He was unsettling in the way he looked at me sideways, like he was estimating my height. I folded my glasses, said goodnight and left. Main Street was quiet. A drunken cowboy walked his pony toward me. It seemed he was having difficulty staying in the saddle, as he rolled forward I stepped out to steady him and, all too late, I saw the grin on his face and felt the jab of something hard in the small of my back. The rider was the man I had hogtied for trapping the raven, and the voice behind the gun at my back was that of Jimmy the Deuce. I felt like Jonesy's rat when confronted with a rattler.

'This is a sawed-off twelve gauge, Bassett, loaded with double ought buck, and you so much as move towards that fancy Colt on your hip and I will happily blow you in half. Happily, you understand that?'

I nodded and raised my hands.

'Put your hands down. We do not want to attract attention. Step back here into the shadows. Jerry, get his gun, and be careful: he is a tricky sonofabitch.'

The man called Jerry reached out and removed my gun. I did not even twitch, although every inch of me wanted to. Sometimes you just know that hole card is the one-eyed jack of hearts when you really need the ace of spades.

Jimmy Olds jabbed the shotgun in a little harder than was necessary to get me moving. 'The Drover's Club it is then, boys,' I said, cheerfully. 'But easy with that shotgun, because when this is over – and it will be over – I am going to shove it up your fat ass, Jimmy the Deuce.'

One-Eyed Jack Temple opened the door to Olds' knock. He smiled at me and took my Colt, offered him by the man called Jerry. 'That will be all, boys. Go get yourselves a drink. I will let you know when Mr Vagg is leaving.'

'You sure, Mr Temple?'

'Very sure. Goodnight.' He closed the door behind them, smiled some more and handed me back my Colt. 'Try not to shoot anyone this night or I might get fired. Come, follow me.'

He led me through to a larger room: a dining room with the remains of what looked to be fine supper spread out on the table. A woman was seated at the head of the table, an unlit cheroot in her hand. I reached into my vest pocket and, crossing the room, pulled out a blue top, thumb lit it and held it for her. She leaned forward and looked at me straight in the eye as she did so, drawing deep and blowing the smoke out of the side of her mouth and not at me as I expected.

'A man with manners at last. You and Jack here seem to be the only two in this godforsaken town.' She offered me her hand and I took it. 'Margaret Vagg. You can call me Margo, but never Marge.'

I gave her my winning smile. 'Pleasure to meet you, Margo.'

'Can I offer you a drink while we are waiting for my brother, Mr Bassett?'

I nodded.

'Whiskey or wine, sir?'

'Whiskey would do just fine, thank you.'

She poured me a generous measure from a crystal decanter, but I supposed it would have tasted just as good from the bottle. A small side door opened and a very frail man stepped into the room and surveyed it carefully before stepping out of the shadows. Frank Vagg was not very tall and his white suit hung on his bones like a drooping flag on a still day. He was of undetermined age, probably not as old as he looked. His skull-like head was framed in wisps of grey hair, and were it not for the shining black eyes then he could have been mistaken for a walking dead man. He moved towards me and held out his hand. It was moist, cold and limp in mine and I felt an urge to dash from the room and wash away the dampness transferred to mine in that brief moment of contact.

'Forgive me for the heavy-handedness of your invitation, Mr Bassett, but time is time and it passes so quickly at my age. I do have need to speak with you tonight and I do not frequent saloons on any occasion. You do understand, I hope.' His voice was little above a whisper.

'No, not really,' I said, sipping my drink and looking beyond him to where One-Eyed Jack Temple had stationed himself by the door, I assumed in readiness for any threat to his employer's health.

'It is really very simple, Mr Bassett.' Margaret Vagg got to her feet and refreshed my glass. 'We would very much like you to come and work for us. Mr Temple here regards you as the right man for the job at hand.'

'I will handle this, Marge,' Vagg interrupted her.

'Well, then for goodness sake, get on with it. I am sure Mr Bassett has other things to do: shoot someone or beat them up or whatever it is he does best. Call me when you are agreed and we can take coffee and maybe a little champagne. Do you like champagne, Mr Bassett?'

I did not answer her but spoke directly to Vagg. I could see this irritated her and I thought *to hell with them both.*

'You have shown yourself to be very capable at handling difficult men, sir, and I have several such men in my employ.' The thin man fixed me with his dark eyes. 'I am trying to run a cattle ranch, conduct business with the Mexicans and secure a future that is fitting and beneficial for all but alas, in some areas, I seem to be wanting. Mr Temple here tells me you know of such matters and would be a great and well-paid asset to my organisation. Are you interested?'

I set my empty glass on the table and declined a refill. 'I have had a look around your organisation, Mr Vagg. A bunch of border trash, mostly: idle men who don't know one end of a steer from the other. Your range is awash with unbranded cattle feeding on bad pasture when there is good grass to be had. Your fences are down and mostly these roughnecks sit around playing cards, drinking or killing wild birds for fun.'

'A harsh judgement, sir.'

'I wouldn't take your coin if I was down to my last dollar, and I am a long way from being that.'

'I take that as a no then, Mr Bassett. Pity, I admire your abilities but not your intellect, which is probably only one step above those you so readily choose to judge. You are a fool, sir.'

'I have great faith in fools. Self-confidence, my friends call it,' I said.

'And you are very well read. Edgar Allen Poe, I believe. An even bigger fool.'

I turned to Margaret Vagg who was, sparingly, smiling at the exchange. I picked up my hat and bowed slightly toward her. 'Thank you for your hospitality, Ma'am; I hope we meet again sometime.'

'As do I, Mr Bassett,' she said softly, and I could see the implied intimacy of the exchange annoyed the hell out of her brother.

I nodded to Temple but ignored Frank Vagg and said quietly, 'I have some business to attend to in the Red Diamond. Come midnight you may well be two men down on the trash you employ.' I turned and left them with those words. Only Jack Temple acknowledged my departure. I was a happy man.

CHAPTER FIFTEEN

A COLD BEER AND HOT LEAD

I believe in meeting trouble head on, and Jimmy the Deuce was trouble for me. I knew that I had to put an end to it; better it be sooner on my terms than maybe later on his from some dark alley. Releasing the hammer strap, I checked the loads in my Colt, put a couple of cotton plugs in my ears and walked across the dark street to the Red Diamond. It was a hot night and the double doors were open; there was still a sprinkling of customers drinking their nightcaps, thirsty or simply too reluctant to call it a night. Mort Cullis and the barber were exactly where I had left them and Billy Bob was at his usual table playing dominoes. A man in a straw hat and striped vest was playing the out-of-tune piano. The man called Jerry and his friend Jimmy Olds were standing in the centre and saw me in the long mirror. Both men froze.

It happens like that. The piano fell silent, conversation dried up and men moved out of the line of fire, seeming to know what was about to go down. I supposed Jimmy and Jerry had been bragging on how they rousted me.

Billy Bob set his counter down and leaned back in his chair. 'Evening, Mr Bassett.'

'Evening, Sheriff. Maybe it would be best if you went fishing.'

He smiled and shook his head. 'Don't fish at night, son. You never know what might creep up behind you.'

'A wise man,' I said, and I meant it.

I turned my attention toward my two captors, noting that Olds still had the shotgun with him; it was propped against the bar near to his left leg. Jerry was visibly trembling but Olds held still, his hand inches from his gun, a look of uncertainty carved into his heavily jowled face. 'Well, boys, what is it to be? You are both packing, so I do not see a problem here if I shoot you both down.'

'Just like that?' Olds said. 'You just shoot us down in a room full of witnesses, including the law.'

'I will give you a chance to pull first, but I warned you once and I never rattle twice.'

Jerry raised his right arm and unbuckled his gun belt with his left, letting it fall at his feet and, stepping clear of the leather, he moved swiftly to one side. 'I'm not going to fight with you, Bassett. I was just obeying orders.'

How many times do you need to hear those words in a lifetime? I wondered. 'I guess it's down to you then, Jimmy. You do have a choice here, though, and I want you to give it some serious thought. Draw or drop your pants, as I aim to put the barrels of that sawed-off you stuck in my back where the sun definitely does not shine.'

'The hell I will.' He growled and pulled.

Same result as the first time: too slow by a heap, and I put a round through his left shoulder and was tempted to follow that with his other ear. He was side on, though, so I let the urge pass. The force of the heavy round bounced him back against the unpolished bar, his foot caught in the rail and he fell heavily, knocking a spittoon clear across the room to rest at Billy Bob's feet. The air reverberated with the echo of the single shot. The powder smoke would leave a stink for a few days and the ears of onlookers would ring for an hour or two, but not mine. I holstered the Colt with a twirl and fished the little cotton bundles out of my ears and dropped them on to the sawdust floor.

The old sheriff nodded approval and did the same, saying, 'I thought you might be calling.'

I looked at Jerry. The man was visibly shaken; twice in only a few days he had come under my gun and I wondered if he was going to stand or run. 'Get him to the doc, Jerry, and remember: either of you ever see me again, it will be for the last time.'

Mort Cullis said, 'Doc's out of town but I do a little

patching up when he's not around. Take him over to my place, Jerry, but keep him in the front of the shop. I got a ripe one out back, a farmer. Awaiting approval from the sheriff here before I plant him.'

Billy Bob waved his hand dismissively and said, 'Bury him, Mort. I forgot clean about him.'

'And send the doctoring bill to Frank Vagg,' I said. 'Add a couple of bucks to it for a round of drinks here and now.'

Someone whooped happily and I ordered two cold beers without heads, one for me and one for Billy Bob Hunt.

As soon as Jerry, Jimmy the Deuce and the undertaker had left, I picked up the sawed-off shotgun. It was an English gun; a lovely piece with a smooth polished walnut stock and what was left of once deeply blued choked barrels. I removed the loads and put them on the table in front of Billy Bob. I tested the hammers: slick but a little heavy on the trigger pull. I put the gun on the table in front of the sheriff. 'You see that Frank Vagg gets that for me, Billy Bob.'

'I'll deliver it myself. Any message with it?'

'Yes. Tell him if any more of his hired trash come after me, I will come straight for him.'

'Just who are you, Mr Bassett?'

'Just a tired man passing through.' I finished my beer, said goodnight and left him with that thought.

I remembered that Joshua Beaufort had once told me that it was better to kill an angry man than humiliate him. I think I hit it somewhere between the two choices, and I left the Red Diamond thinking of Henri Larsson and wondered if she had heard the shooting. If so, did she think that I might be involved?

CHAPTER SIXTEEN

THE DEVIL

It was late by the time I returned to the hotel. I needed a meal, a bath and a clean shirt. The smell of black powder smoke clings to a man's clothes long after the hammer drops and the round is capped. I ate a thick steak, washed it down with black coffee in the empty hotel dining room and waited while the disgruntled hired man stoked the boiler that heated the water in the steamy warmth of the Wayfarer's bathhouse. I gave him four bits for his late night's work, which brought a smile to his sour face. Fine how half a dollar can bring the light back into a tired old man's eyes. I soaked for an hour, smoking a cheroot and sipping from a fifth of whiskey, nodding my approval as he topped up the hot water. Then mellow, hot and wrapped in the hired red bathrobe that went along with the cost of the bath, and carrying my clothes, I made my way up the backstairs to my room and settled on the bed. Damn Texas and its weather: one night it's chillingly cold or boiling hot, and the next the air is damp and humid extracting moisture from every pore; more uncomfortable than being in a Sioux sweat lodge.

I had just reached that sleepy stage where reality turns into a distant dream when the knock on my door forced me to the surface and back into the world I would like to have left for an hour or two. I thought to ignore it but the tapping became insistent, and I rolled off the bed, picked up the Derringer and shuffled barefoot to the door.

'God, Lucas, I thought you were dead.' Henri Larsson stared at me, that mischief alive in her dark eyes. She shook her head slowly and, closing the door behind her and leaning back on it, said, 'Do you ever come to the door with your actual clothes on and without your pistol in your hand?'

She was laughing at me but I was too tired to care.

'Depends,' I said, setting the little gun on the night-stand.

'On what?' she said.

'On who is knocking,' I said.

'Sorry if I woke you.'

'That's OK; you did not. Just dozing, is all. Drink?'

'No, thank you.' She stared at me for a long while and I flopped back onto the bed. 'Was that gunfight really necessary?' she asked, her voice quiet, a little husky.

102

'You heard about that already?'

'I would guess the whole town has heard about it. Well, was it?' There was a sharp, irritable edge to her voice.

'I do not know for sure, but I am fed up with San Pedro and would like to be on my way back to Wyoming, where the weather is more predictable. Nothing here worth getting shot for. Vagg offered me a job and I turned it down, is all.'

'Wouldn't it have been a smart move to get inside of his organisation?'

'He hasn't got an organisation, just a raggle-taggle crew of trigger-happy low-lives.'

'That how you read it?'

'That's how I read it. Look, Henri: Frank Vagg is a greedy old man who looks like he should have died years ago. He is buying up the bottomland to the east of the town in the hope of – or on bought intelligence – that the Denver and Rio Grande will choose that route and make him a very wealthy man. It's not a new story by any means and it is one the US Marshals can handle; no need for Pinkerton agents to be involved. You can write that in your weekly report to San Antonio, I can get paid and we can both go home: me to Wyoming and you back to civilization.'

It was some speech and my throat was dry. 'If you're not having a drink, you can pour me one. My feet ache.'

She stared at me long and hard. 'You really believe that is it?'

'Yes, I do really believe that is it.'

She poured me a generous measure, brought it over to the bed and settled on the side as I shifted over. 'I think there is more to it than that, Lucas. Margaret Vagg has been sending telegraphs to a bank in San Antonio, from what I hear on the key; innocent enough in their content but each one carries the word Diablo. Do you know what Diablo means?'

'It's the Mex word for the Devil, is all.'

'No, I mean in this context.'

'No. Do you? Probably some code word to a fancy Dan banker she's got on her line. I hear she spends a lot of time there and I cannot say that I blame her for that.'

'Maybe and maybe not; I think I will make it a query in my report to Beaufort.'

'Report away, just so long as it gets us out of here. Anything else you are worried about?'

'One of Vagg's men brought in several wires today, mostly to suppliers, but one was to a man in Bitter Springs, New Mexico, asking for him to make contact regarding employment. It was too fast for me to get the whole thing.'

'Who was this man? He have a name?'

'Max Hadley.'

I quickly sat up straight and spilt some of my drink in the process.

'Max Hadley,' I said. 'Damn the man.'

'You know him. . . ?'

'Yes; but worse than that, Agent Larsson, he knows

me and what I do for a living, which means he will guess who you are and our job here will be done whether we want it to be or not.'

'Where do you know him from?'

'A south Texas shithole called Dry Water about five hundred miles to the east of here. He was a lawman on the wrong side of the law, and I put him right. He tried to foul me up with the Wyoming law enforcement but Marshal Beaudine straightened that out. The man lost his job and I left town with him in jail nursing a bad headache and a gimp I had given him as a leaving present.'

'Did you break the case?'

'Yes, with Jake Benbow's help. It was pretty bloody.'

'Was it bad?'

'It cost Agent Kathleen Riley her life when she got too close to the dingus and I didn't have her back well enough to protect her.'

Henri slid off the bed, walked over to the small table and poured herself a long drink, holding it to her breast and staring out into the darkness. Finally, she turned back toward me, set her glass down and walked over to the bed. 'Do you like me, Lucas Santana? I mean, really like me?'

'Yes,' I said. 'Very much. Too much, perhaps.'

'Never too much, Lucas.' She settled down beside me and, undoing the top buttons of her blouse, took my hand and guided me to her breasts, then leaned forward and brushed my lips with hers, saying, 'I'll follow thee and make a heaven of hell.'

She looked up at me and I said, 'To die upon the hand I love so well. . . .'

I laughed quietly; Henri Larsson was also well read.

Later, in the darkness and the quiet time that follows a burst of passion, a sometimes foolish burst of love making, Henri turned on her side to face me. I knew it was a retrospective grilling, a habit some women have, of committing themselves without question and then trying to back up that impulse to prove to themselves it was the right decision to make. This is a problem most men do not seem to have. 'How old are you, Lucas Santana?' she asked, her voice husky, almost a whisper.

I thought about the answer to that, and I did not have one. 'I don't actually know,' I said. 'Somewhere maybe a little more or a little short of forty-five, but a good shade less than fifty. I have often wondered the answer to that question myself.'

She raised herself onto one elbow; her face was cupped in her left hand and she pulled my face towards her with the other. 'You have to be fooling with me. A detective who does not even know how old he is?'

'It's a fact,' I said, staring up at the ceiling. 'I was a foundling, taken in by a Montana lawman and his wife. They gave me a home, their good name and their love but they had no idea who I was, how old I was or where I came from. They guessed maybe three or four years old and started from there.'

'When did they tell you?'

'When I was twelve.'

'Did you ever wonder where your real folks were?'

'Hard to get that information; records were a little scarce back then and, in any case, as far as I was concerned the Santanas were my folks. Jesse Santana taught me when to pull a trigger and when to walk away, and Miriam taught me how to live a decent life. I hope I have lived up to her expectations. She was a frontier woman, a lawman's wife and she knew there would be bridges, lines if you will, for me to cross.'

'Are they still alive?'

'No, sadly they passed while I was serving.'

'The blue or the grey?'

'The Confederacy; Hood's Texas Brigade.'

She kissed my cheek and snuggled up against me as I studied the ceiling again and drifted off to sleep. When I awoke she was gone and I stared at the ceiling some more, wondering if Annie Blue would approve of my actions. I had that sure feeling that she would. Being in my line of work, we had often talked about such things, both of us knowing that one time I might not come back but be buried in some lonesome grave far from the Wildcat and her. Life goes on.

CHAPTER SEVENTEEN

MAX HADLEY

'Playtime is over. I tried the easy way, but Bassett is an arrogant and impertinent bastard. Rousted one of the boundary riders and threatened to kill him over a god-damned raven blind. He beat up on one of my men and shot another's ear off and then shot him again tonight and threatened me. Had the nerve to send my shotgun back with Billy Bob Hunt. He showed no respect whatsoever to Margaret. Time to take the man down. Are you up for that, Jack?'

Temple thought about it long and hard. Being Vagg's bodyguard was an excellent job; looking out for his business interest within accepted parameters was also good, and both jobs were well rewarded, but murder. . . . That was not part of his job description.

'No, sir, Mr Vagg. He came at you with intent to harm. That would be one thing, but his rousting a couple of the border trash you have working for you, and not showing you the respect you merit. . . . Well, that is another matter.'

'You scared of him or what?'

'No, sir, I've studied some on the man and I think I could take him. It would be close and it would have to be for the right reason, and you have not given me one. I'll draw my pay if you want it that way.'

'No, I don't want that. Jack, you are one independent cuss and I respect you for that. One of the reasons I like and trust you, in fact; reminds me of me at another time and place. It's also one of the reasons I don't involve you in what some might think to be the darker side to our enterprise here on the Circle V. I won't put you on the spot, Jack. I have already sent for a man some weeks ago and since confirmed my offer in a wire in the last couple of days, in fact. He's a man who will do the job in hand: one with your rep but not your scruples. He can handle it. He will cost, but Bassett is an itch I need to scratch permanent.'

Max Hadley considered the letter and the telegraph that followed it at some length. It was interesting, and he could smell money – a lot of money – and money was his game. He was a big man, over six foot, with long black hair and a fashionable drooping moustache on a darkly tanned face that carried a white scar from temple to the edge of his lower lip. He dressed in

109

black, walked with a slight limp and wore a tied down sidearm on his right hip.

It was an offer, should he prove to be suitable, to work as a trouble-shooter on a large ranch on the Texas/Mexican border. The owner, Frank Vagg, had stressed that he had been recommended by friends, who had found his services in the past to be satisfactory with their duties fulfilled. Recognising the names of the previous employers told Hadley all that he needed to know about what kind of job was on offer.

Bitter Creek was dead. He would be happy to see the back of it, and the people who lived there probably as much as they would be of him. As the town council's appointed marshal, his heavy-handed dealings with even minor lawbreakers had not gone down well. That and the fact most of any fines levied somehow did not find their way into the town's coffers. He answered the telegraph immediately, dropped his badge and a brief letter of resignation on to the office desk, packed his bag and by midday was well on his way to a town called San Pedro on the south Texas/Mexican border. He arrived just forty-eight hours after leaving Bitter Creek and, by dusk on the following day, he was astride a hired horse. With directions gained from the liveryman, he was headed for the Circle V.

Frank Vagg and his sister Margaret were taking a sundowner on the back porch of the Circle V with the albino gunman Val Lefranc. Jack Temple walked the

limping Max Hadley through the house and intro-
duced the big man to his prospective employer.

Vagg got to his feet unsteadily, shook hands and sat
back down again quickly. He was feeling rough following the previous evening's bout of drinking mescal
followed foolishly by a peyote button: not a great com-
bination. 'Good of you to come, Mr Hadley. A pleasant
journey, I hope. Rain washed out the Overland trail
last week, but I understand the road to be passable
again.'

'Already dusty, Mr Vagg. This country dries the
moisture out of just about anything and everything,
including humans.'

'Very true, sir. Very true. This is my sister, Margaret,
and her companion Val Lefranc. You have already met
my friend, Jack Temple. Margaret, will you please pour
our guest a drink. Whiskey, I assume, Mr Hadley?'

Hadley shook hands with the woman, holding it
longer than was necessary, nodded to Temple and
took the chair offered, watching carefully as the one-
eyed man and the albino both retired to distant seats
by the porch doorway.

'You come highly recommended, sir,' Vagg said,
sipping his lemonade. 'My friends both north and
south of the border assure me you are the man for the
job outlined briefly in my letter.'

'No problem, if the money is still there to back the
offer.'

'I assure you it is, Max. May I call you Max?' He did
not wait for a reply. 'Three hundred dollars a month,

111

and found of course. We keep a good table and cellar here on the Circle V.'

'Sounds fair; getting a bunch of drifters to toe the party line is not a problem as long as I have a free hand to deal with them as I choose.'

'They are restless and bored at present, but shortly they will be doing the job they were actually hired on for. Currently they are encouraging the small ranchers – nesters, homesteaders, call them what you will – to move on with a few dollars in their pockets or else possibly be buried there.' He coughed long and hard, wiping his thin lips with a silk handkerchief and, taking another sip of his drink, got to his feet unsteadily. 'Margaret will explain all that you need to know at present about our major project and show you to your room here in the main building. But I, Max, am weary and will retire for my rest, and if you have no questions, we will assume your contract to be in order.'

Max Hadley was in no hurry for bed.

'One thing, Mr Vagg: I don't like to walk into trouble blind. You mentioned one particular problem that will need my attention immediately, and that would be. . . ?'

Vagg paused, looked at Jack Temple, and said, 'There is a man in town. A troublesome drifter arrived recently and he has proved to be a pain in the ass. Mr Temple here, my bodyguard and friend, is reluctant to deal with him for very personal reasons, but I think once you have surveyed the territory then that man should be you first objective.'

'This drifter have a name?'

'We believe it to be Louis Bassett of Wichita, but that may not be so. The local law thinks he might be the Peaceful River Kid. A foolish name if I ever heard one; the man must be over forty years old.'

Hadley set down his drink. 'Describe this Louis Bassett to me.'

Vagg gave an irritable cough and sat back down, thinking. 'About five ten or eleven tall. He's lean, dark haired, but greying at the temples with a close-trimmed moustache. Wears a fancy Colt in a cross-draw holster. Strange man; seems to have a penchant for ravens. I would like him dead.'

Margaret Vagg said, a chuckle on the very edge of her deep voice, 'Don't forget his lovely blue eyes, Frank; they have seen a lot of yesterdays.'

'But not too many more tomorrows, I hope.' Vagg said.

Hadley whistled, sat back in his seat and laughed.

'What's so funny?' Vagg asked, his voice agitated.

'You want that man dead, it will cost you an extra five hundred.'

'Why would that be?' Vagg asked after a long silence.

'That man is not Louis Bassett of Wichita. That man is Lucas Santana, a sometime Pinkerton agent and deputy US Marshal. He gave me this limp in a dirty little town called Dry Water, and I have tried before to put him in the ground without success. The man is almost bullet proof. You want him dead? It will cost you.'

113

'Are you absolutely certain of those facts? A detective, a federal officer?'

'No question.'

'That could prove disastrous for everyone, ruin everything.' Vagg's tight skinned white forehead crinkled with a worried frown. 'Damn the man; put him down.'

'And the five hundred?'

'You certainly do not come cheap, Mr Hadley,' Vagg whispered.

'No, sir, I do not. That man is going to be hard to kill. He seems to like critters more than human beings. Has himself a small ranch in Wyoming called the Wildcat. It's posted land. Wyoming, no hunting, would you believe that?'

'It is settled, then,' Vagg said, getting to his feet unsteadily and nodding to Jack Temple. 'Give me your arm, Jack. I need some fresh air before bed. Margaret, I'll leave you to outline the Diablo Project as far as it concerns Mr Hadley, but only as far as it concerns Mr Hadley. Leave the rest of it to me. We will see how things work out first.'

'What do you think of him, Jack?' Vagg asked once they were clear of the room and smoking late night smokes: Vagg a cheroot and Temple a quirly.

'Just another hired gun, smarter than most and better dressed, maybe, but underneath all that is just a cheap gunman who will likely take Bassett or whatever his name is from some dark alley.'

114

'Bassett is a threat; you have to admit that.'

'Hadley may turn out to be a bigger one further down the pike.'

'To me?'

'You can never tell with a man like that.'

'Then you had best keep your eye on him, Jack.'

CHAPTER EIGHTEEN

RIDER FROM
THE PAST

After what turned out to be another pretty fruitless day checking on the possible homestead Henri had staked out for me, and surveying even more of the rugged countryside, I headed back to San Pedro. It was clear to me that I would not learn anything more by continually pounding my backside on hard leather. Any thoughts of using the homestead as a base were dismissed at first sight of the place; it had been torched. Only the stone-set chimney still stood as a testimony to the long, backbreaking hours of arduous work put into the place by a dreamer – a man, or a family from the east, perhaps – with bright hopes for a future along the mighty Rio Grande. I wondered just how many dreams Frank Vagg had shattered during his long life.

The sky was a blaze of deep red as I stabled the Morgan. The coal oil street lamps were lit and flickering in the light breeze, but the street was deserted and the only lights burning were in the saloon and the hotel. Even the diner and billiard hall were closed. It was a Monday and not uncommon for a town to take a long sleep after a busy weekend. I walked the tired Morgan into the grey light of the livery, unsaddled her, rubbed her down, fed her some grain and checked the water. I arched my back, massaged my backside and turned toward the door. My hand dropped to my Colt as the dark figure of One-Eyed Jack Temple emerged from the deeper shadow.

'Easy, partner. I like a man who cares for his animal.'

I leaned back on one of the stalls, took my pipe from my shirt pocket and filled it; it made a change from cheap cigars and quirlys. 'A man needs to be careful, Jack; you know that.'

The big man set himself down on a straw bale, extracted a tailormade from a leather case and lit it.

'That's why I am here, Kid. You have come a long way since that night in Cheyenne, but it seems you left a trail behind you, and this one leads back to a town called Dry Water. You remember that?'

'Not a happy memory, Jack.'

'You recall a *hombre* named Max Hadley? White scar on his face and walks with a limp?'

117

'I remember him; I gave him the limp to remember me by. I think Old Nick gave him the scar.'

'That may not have been a smart move; sometimes it's better to kill a man than to shame him.'

'Good advice; someone else gave it me onetime and I do not doubt it, but now, as then, a couple of years too late.'

'He arrived at the Circle V yesterday. Vagg is planning on having him as his top hand.'

'Hadley doesn't know one end of a cow from the other.'

'That may be so, but he surely knows you, though. He enlightened us somewhat as to your Pinkerton career and other attachments to federal law enforcement. The Vaggs were not impressed or best pleased.'

'And you, Jack, how do you feel about it?'

Temple shrugged. 'What I feel does not really matter. Those people mean to do you harm, Kid, maybe more than even you can handle.' He smiled a crinkled smile and pushed the patch up onto his forehead, rubbed the eye, blinked hard and dropped it down again.

'And you?'

'I'm on my way to New Orleans. I like that old river. I figured if I stayed around here, it would only be a matter of time before Vagg asked me to help Hadley take you down, and I am not too sure I am that good. Hadley will do you from cover and that is not my style.'

'You could stay and help.'

'Not my style, either. I took Vagg's coin and I will

not go against him, but I will tell you this, Kid: stay away from Diablo Canyon. I do not know for sure what is going down there below the line, but I feel a darkness about it whenever it is mentioned.'

'What do you think?' I asked.

'I think things are never quite how they seem.'

'Like people,' I said.

'Yes, just like people. You behind a badge: who would have believed that?' He dropped the stub of his cigarette onto the dirt floor and ground it out with his boot heel. He turned his back on me and disappeared into a stall, and remerged leading a big bay, saddled and loaded with bedroll, a war bag and draping duster.

'So long, Kid. I guess we will meet again. In the meantime, you watch your back. Sometime maybe I will visit you at your Wildcat ranch up there on the Peaceful.'

'How do you know it's called Wildcat?'

'Hadley told us. Seems he knows one hell of a lot about you.'

That needed thinking about.

We shook hands and he gave me a scrap of paper with a couple of scribbled lines on it. 'If you are ever down by the Big River, look me up: that address will find me. We'll maybe share a beer and talk about old times.'

I watched as he swung his tall frame into the saddle, touched his wide-brimmed hat and rode out into the starlit Texas night, Louisiana and the Mississippi bound.

She was waiting in the darkness of my room for me, standing by the window, silhouetted against the dying evening red sky.

I tossed my hat and saddlebags on the bed and said, 'I locked the door. How did you get in?'

'Picked the lock; very simple.'

'Why have you always bothered to knock?'

'More ladylike.'

'This the sort of thing Beaufort is teaching his female agents in San Antonio, how to pick locks?'

'That, and how to drink whiskey. They teach us a lot at the agency.'

I took the hint and poured us a pair, passing one to her. Our eyes met briefly and she did not blink as I started to turn away. 'You are a Mr Grumpy this evening. Are you regretting what happened last night? Because I am not.'

I gave her a tired smile, stepped closer and touched her cheek with my fingertips, dancing them along her cheekbone and gently brushing her lips with them before turning away.

'What troubles you, Lucas? Are you confusing me with Kathleen Riley? If so, do not.'

'You are an astute young woman, Henri, and I want like hell to hold you, but I cannot afford to. My soul could not take the weight of losing someone else as close to me as you have quickly become. Maybe when this is over . . .' My words tailed off and dried up. *When this is over,* I thought to myself, *more dead men and perhaps even me among them.* Would these kinds of days ever be over for me? More to the point, did I actually want them to be?

'I heard from Beaufort today.' Her voice was suddenly very businesslike and pitched slightly higher than it had been only moments before. Her words broke my reverie.

'And?' I said.

'He knows, or thinks he knows, what Diablo means.'

'Gold?' I said.

There was a hint of a smile as her voice softened again. Two agents on the job, the night before between the cool sheets of my bed put on one side. 'It's always gold, isn't it? It seems to be the grease that lubricates the bearings of this country and is probably the main reason we are needed. Power and gold: either way, one buys the other, always.'

'How much are we talking about, Henri?' I asked.

'Only the Mexican government or, to be more precise, only President Porfirio Diaz can answer that question.'

'Is he getting ready to run?'

'Beaufort doesn't think so; simply moving some of his eggs from one basket to another just in case.'

'From where to where?'

'Mexico City to San Antonio.'

'And Diablo?'

'A canyon to the south of here; it's on the Mex side of the border and on the eastern side of San Pedro.

Moving it by pack mule, escorted by army or *federales* all of the way to San Antonio by special dispensation from Washington. Seems *el president* may invest a large chunk of it in stock for the Denver and Rio Grande Railway, which, by the way, again according to intel gathered by Beaufort, will not be coming this way but much further to the west.'

'To El Paso.'

'Very likely.'

'That will make our friend Vagg very unhappy.'

'You think he is going to try for the gold?'

'I do. He has a small army littered around the Circle V, enough I would think to handle an ambush in Diablo Canyon. Map it for me and I will take a looksee tomorrow. You happy to hold the fort?'

'Beaufort will be here by the time you return. He wants to be hands on with this one; he aims to stop it before it begins. Apparently Washington will not be happy if this gets out of hand. I think he plans to ride out and meet the gold shipment before there is any real trouble.'

'That might be a greater task that he bargains for,' I said.

She nodded. 'Does that bother you? Him taking over, I mean.'

'Not in the least. I am a hired hand, a mercenary, not even a full-time agent such as yourself. It's his call, and when the bugle sounds, I march.'

'You, sir, are a liar.'

I laughed. I could not help myself. I reached out for

her and pulled her to me, kissing her softly on her lips, feeling them part briefly as she pushed me away, and then pulled me back to her again. Women. . . . Why must they always feel the need to be in charge?

CHAPTER NINETEEN

BILLY BOB HUNT

It was typically seasonal Texas weather: a few days burning you black, the rising heat creating thunder and rain, and the cycle beginning all over again when that had passed. It was passing now and I was in the dry for a change. I had been in San Pedro for two weeks, and in that time I had shot the same man twice: first time taking off his ear and the second time sorely wounding him. I had nearly crippled another with my boot, insulted the head honcho, and freed a raven. I had seduced or been seduced by a fellow agent near young enough for me to be her father, drunk several fifths of whiskey and conjured up a man from the past who hated my guts. And now, having been on the wrong trail for the most of that time, I was about to be play second fiddle to the agent in charge. So much for Lucas Santana: private detective. I was pondering these things over my coffee, following a scrambled egg on toast breakfast in the Blue Parrot, when Billy Bob Hunt walked through the open doorway. He hung his dripping slicker on a peg and beat his rain-soaked derby against his leg, bending it back into shape and sitting it back on his grey head. He settled his eyes on me and walked over to my table and, without being invited, pulled a chair and thumped his hefty backside down on to it with a sigh and a smile.

'Any objections?' he asked.

I shook my head.

'Mind if I smoke?' he asked, pulling a stogie from his vest pocket.

Again, I shook my head.

'This going to be a one-sided conversation?'

I shrugged and poured some sugar into my coffee cup.

'OK then, shall I do the talking?'

'What's on your mind, Sheriff?'

'Just this morning I got a letter from Tad Jones up in Sentinel. We go back a'ways, Tad and I. He doesn't think too highly of me, I know, but we are kind of neighbours and I guess he feels guilty about something.'

'Something?'

'Yes, something, like holding out on me and sicking a federal backed detective on my trail.'

'Interesting.'

'Damned right, it is, but I've been a lawman long enough to know you are not who you make yourself out to be. Just wish you had given me the chance to let you know I am not a fancy badge carrier for a high roller like Frank Vagg. I'm past retirement and if I turn my back now and again, it isn't for money: it's for a quiet and, I hope, longer life.'

'And you are telling me this . . . why?'

'Why, because if there is a way to clean up this burg without getting my ass shot off, then I would like to be in on it and get out from under Vagg's thumb. But damn it, I don't want to horn in where I am not wanted.' His face got a little red and his eyes a little brighter as he stood up and pushed his chair back, staring down at me.

'Sit down and shut up, Billy Bob.' I waved to the waitress. 'Two more coffees please, miss.'

He sat staring at me for a long while over his coffee and I waited. I have found the best thing to do with an angry man when you sense that that man does not really want to be angry is to be patient and let the storm pass quietly.

'I was town marshal here for three years, employed by the town council before Vagg came along. Riverton is one small county and he got me elected county sheriff. I could have said no, but my age ruled out my starting over, so I took it but I never took anything other than my fair wages. Like I said, it was safer to go fishing now and then. It never bothered me if they shot one another, just so long as the towns-

126

folk were not harmed.'

'And the settlers, the onetime owners of the deserted homesteads littered about the place?'

'You are right, and I always will feel bad about that, but I wasn't about to die for something that has been happening all over Texas since the end of the war, and that was a long time back.'

'And now?'

'Now, I'm tired of it all.' He stood up, calmer than the first time, and pushed his chair await from the table gently. 'I can ride and I am better than most with a Winchester: you need me, you holler.'

He started to turn for the door, but I reached out and touched his shoulder. As he turned I offered him my hand and said quietly, 'Lucas Santana. I'm the Pinkerton man Tad told you about, and for the record, he did not speak ill of you.'

'Thanks for that,' he said, gripping my hand before turning back toward the door.

I watched as he shrugged into the long mackinaw before touching his battered hat and walking out into the pouring rain. I wondered what it must have been like, being in his situation at his late age, and I did not envy him his conscience or condemn his reaction to it. A man can only do so much, and knowing your limitations is a vital part of survival in a place where you might find yourself to be the only badge around.

Two days later, Joshua Beaufort and Jacob Benbow arrived on the early evening stage. I watched from my hotel window as they approached the Wayfarers, both men tall and erect, parade ground backbones, military through and through.

CHAPTER TWENTY

DIABLO CANYON MASSACRE

It began at six o'clock in the morning with cold dawning, hours before the full sun would bless the canyon bottom and before the grey rocks warmed for the lizards and snakes to emerge and take it all in. The Mexican soldiers – fifteen troopers and one officer – emerged from their blankets to a cold breakfast of beans and corn bread. No fire and no coffee; they had travelled that way for seven long, hard days and nights. At first, they had been alert: guards were posted with outriders flanking the train, but upon entering Diablo Canyon, things had changed. The outriders were drawn into the narrow passageway and the guards had grown lax and weary. A continuous diet of cold beans and bread are not conducive to discipline for an underpaid, underfed and undervalued soldier. The officer, a young lieutenant, tried to rally his men each morning, but he was under strict orders to run a cold camp until the train had crossed the river. The troopers, he had been informed, would be well fed and treated in San Pedro, where a US cavalry escort would meet them and take the gold on to San Antonio. The US troops would be led by Colonel Frank Vagg, who would see to their every need.

But it was not the false Colonel Vagg who was waiting to meet them long before they emerged at the Rio Bravo, well to the east of San Pedro. High in the broken grey granite, hidden from the escort's view, were twenty outlaws: renegade Yaqui Indians and Mexican border trash, led by Max Hadley and a one-eared man. As the soldiers emerged from a cold night's sleep and wrestled with their restless mounts, and as the four muleskinners reloaded the mules, Hadley dropped his arm, giving the order to fire.

And so, the massacre began. Twenty firearms poured hot lead down into the canyon, catching the mule train and its guardians in a deadly crossfire.

The noise was sudden and stridently shattering as fire poured down, many of the rounds ricocheting, screaming off the granite and mixing with the shrieking of the dead and the dying.

'Fish in a barrel,' Hadley muttered, directing fire as best he could from a vantage point a little above the undisciplined gunmen from the Circle V.

Jimmy the Deuce emptied his Winchester and drew

one of the two Colts he had strapped on. He slithered down the rocks to find a closer killing ground. Hadley watched the big man; they had not seen eye-to-eye since his arrival at the Circle V and his appointment as trouble-shooter, a role Olds himself had cherished. He could be bothersome further down the line. Hadley gave it but a moment's thought; he raised the muzzle of his rifle an inch and shot the big man in the back of the head. Olds fell like a stone, rolled and tumbled down the loose shale to fall across the body of a dying Mexican trooper.

Problem solved, Hadley worked fresh loads in the port of the Winchester, worked the lever and shot the young lieutenant through the heart.

Beaufort mustered us just after daybreak. His intention was that we cross the river, ride hard for Diablo Canyon and meet up with the column before they reached its narrowest part. Then, we would scout ahead and lead them safely through to the Rio, where I had found a safe place for them to bivouac for the night before crossing the heavily laden mules over into San Pedro. But it did not work out that way.

We heard the sound of distant gunfire well before we reached the high ground along the narrow canyon named after the Devil himself. We had just rested the horses: Beaufort and Benbow were astride quickly selected bays, with the newly recruited Billy Bob Hunt on a big black. I had my regular Morgan between my knees.

'That sounds like a mighty big ruckus; we may be too late,' Beaufort said, heeling his mount forward at a gallop. I caught up with him quickly, but young Benbow, not the experienced horseman that we were, brought up the rear with red-faced Billy Bob Hunt riding hard several yards behind him. The clatter of the hoofs muted the sound of the gunfire, and by the time we reached the grey rimrock at the head of the canyon and brought the sweating horses to a stop, it was all over.

Benbow moved to the front and looked down on the bloody scene below.

It had been a deadly ambush and looked as though the mule train had been blasted in a murderous cross-fire. The military escort was scattered: their bodies mostly lay where they had fallen, with several close by to their dead mounts. Others had dispersed but, taking fire from both sides, had nowhere to hide. Two of the mules were down and one still alive was braying in agony. The ambushers, several of whom I recognised from my wanderings as being Circle V hands, were stripping the dead soldiers of anything they considered to be of value, such as personal items and weaponry; the latter included some very saleable items on the frontier. Hadley was examining the contents of one of the strongboxes, which had smashed open as the mule had fallen against a rocky outcrop.

Suddenly the soldier in Jacob Benbow clicked in. Mexican or no, that was no way to treat a fallen warrior. 'Fuck this,' he whispered, almost to himself and, still mounted, shook the Henry from its leather sheath. He shouldered the weapon and, at a good two hundred yards, shot and killed a pair of the looters, with a third round killing the injured mule.

And that was it; nothing left to do but join in. Both Beaufort and I dismounted and, standing, opened fire: he with his Henry and me with my Marlin. Billy Bob stationed himself behind a rock, using it as a rest for his Winchester.

There was panic among the killers. Not knowing where we were, they fired in every direction while we carefully – and with little regret – dropped them one by one where they stood, or where they ran, but not Max Hadley. He would have been my first choice, but at the first of Benbow's rounds he had dived for cover behind a huge slab of granite and I had not seen him since.

'Hold fire,' Beaufort yelled, and again, 'hold fire.'

He was right. It was all over. Only the army horses and uninjured mules were still standing.

Leaving our mounts, but still alert, we climbed down into the canyon. I moved quickly to the shelter of the large rock that had hidden Hadley but there was no sign of the big man. I wondered where they had hidden their horses, but guessed they would be above and well hidden in a terrain that looked as if some giant hand had shattered the landscape and spread the resulting chaos with a single sweep.

'Sorry, Chief,' Benbow said guiltily, thumbing fresh rounds in the tubular magazine of the Henry. 'I just hate to see dead soldiers treated that way.'

'Nothing to be sorry about, Jacob; you were only a second or two ahead of us.' He turned to me, a sad smile on his handsome face. 'That right, Lucas?'

'Almost less than that, son,' I said. 'Almost less than that. Pity we missed Hadley, though; bastard ducked behind a rock before I could nail him.'

'He won't be hard to find,' Beaufort said. He sounded sure of himself, but I was not: Max Hadley was a slippery customer and would do just about everything to protect his hide.

'Jesus Christ,' said the out-of-breath Billy Bob. 'I have never seen the like of this day and never thought I would.'

'Sadly,' Beaufort said, matter-of-factly and almost to himself, 'I have.'

'Gettysburg?' I asked.

He nodded and stared into the middle-distance for a moment, reflecting, I thought, on something best forgotten but impossible to forget. He turned, parade ground stiff and said quietly, 'Let's get to it, boys.'

The hot sun burned down upon us, and my shirt was soaked in sweat. We rounded up the army mounts, stripped those we did not need of all harness and turned them lose, heading them back the way they had come. Benbow found where the ambushers had hidden a dozen of their horses in a small gully and we drove those ahead of us to the river. They all carried the Circle V brand and we guessed they would find their way home from there. We took the packs from the dead mules and transferred them to the saddle horses, one of which did not take kindly to the unaccustomed load, but quietened after some soft words from Beaufort.

'We'll leave the gold in the Wells Fargo strong room in back of the Overland office tomorrow. I will wire head office to send half-a-dozen agents to see it is well guarded until Beaudine can get some military personnel here to escort it through to San Antonio. That is not the agency's responsibility.'

'And the Mexican soldiers?' Benbow asked.

'I will notify the Mexican authorities. We can bring them in for them or they can send a burial party; that will be up to them. In the meantime, we cover them with whatever we can find in their equipment: ponchos, blankets and the like. It's all we can do.'

'And the others?' Billy Bob asked.

'You send word to Frank Vagg where they are,' I said. 'He wants them? He can go and get them. Me, I am happy to leave them be.'

'I'll be pleased to do that,' the old man said, shoving his Winchester back into the saddle boot and repeating the words to himself quietly.

'The ravens will also like that,' I said.

Beaufort looked at me, an unasked question of his lips, but I just smiled, swung aboard the Morgan and took the lead. I led us out that hellhole aptly named Diablo Canyon, looking forward to a quiet supper and a nightcap with Henri Larsson. Strange really, maybe even frightening, but I had shot to death men I had not even bothered to count and I felt absolutely nothing. Perhaps it was time for me to reflect on a different future.

CHAPTER
TWENTY-ONE

DEATH OF A
HIRED GUN

The next day I made an early start for Diablo Canyon.
On the high ground, I passed a contingent of *federales*,
a burial party I guessed, sent by the army and on their
way to reclaim the Mexican dead. I did not believe for
one minute that Frank Vagg would do the same for his
men, although Billy Bob had been tasked with – and
enthusiastically delivered – Beaufort's message.

It took me a good two hours to pick up Max
Hadley's tracks. From the canyon, he had made his
way to a clearing where several horses had been tethered. He had loosed the animals and scattered them. I
estimated from the droppings that there were at least

a half dozen animals, and he had lost his trail among theirs. Eventually I found where he had left them but it was shale-covered ground, making it difficult to follow, but once on it, and moving at a slow and careful pace, I followed it back down towards where the Rio Grande offered a reasonably shallow crossing well to the west of San Pedro. Upriver or down? Two choices. If I got it right first time then it would not be a problem in finding where he had emerged from the green water on the Texas side. Make the wrong choice and it could set me back half a day and mean a cold camp and hard tack for supper. I decided the upstream side and eventually found where he had forded the river.

I followed Hadley's tracks for three long, hot hours to the foot of a rocky escarpment, dismounted and tied off the bay to a dead mesquite. The area was hard and the trail difficult to read, but appeared to be leading me uphill to where a rock-strewn canyon gave way to higher ground, and it was difficult for a horse and rider. There was little to indicate how long the man ahead of me had been riding: no pony droppings and very little vegetation. The sun poured down on us like golden rain, bounced off the grey rocks and hit us again. We were both bathed in sweat and my shirt stuck to my back like a second skin. I stripped off my vest and undershirt and rubbed the animal down with the latter before stowing it in my saddlebag, taking a swig of warm water from my last canteen and giving her most of the last of it in my hat. She snorted the water at me and I poured what was left over my head. I squatted down on my haunches, rolled a cigarette and examined the ground with a great care. The faint trail was lost in the shale.

I studied on the problem for some time. No point in going forward blind, so I decided my best move was to go back to the lower ground and refill the canteens from the last waterhole. I had passed it a few days before when scouting the terrain, so I was pretty sure there would still be water, and there was. Walking, I led the Morgan and heard her snort at the smell of the water. It was cool and about a foot deep, left over from the recent rain drained down from the distant mountains. The bay quickened her pace and I let her walk past me.

The ground around the waterhole was sandy and bereft of any animal prints, which was strange: it was almost as if the ground had been swept clear. I knelt for a closer look and saw the discarded mesquite branch far too late to do much about it.

I was so intent on my own observation, in fact, that I failed to hear the approaching man until it was also too late. My enthusiasm, my desire to bring the man down had made me careless; he had also doubled back and was behind me.

A greenhorn would have known better.

'While you are down there, you piece of shit, you'd best say a prayer. If you so much as fart, I will cut you in half.'

I turned slowly and looked up into the cold, dead

stare of the pale-eyed Max Hadley. His face red, either from the heat, exertion or the excitement – it was hard to tell – but the white scar seemed to stand out against the red flesh of his face like a thin white snake, more clearly so than I had ever seen it. The man had doubled back over his trail knowing I would be totally absorbed in my own difficult progress to note the lack of his. An amateur's mistake and one I appeared to be about to pay for with my life. The sawed-off shotgun in his big hands was Vagg's lightweight English piece: the one I had taken from Jimmy the Deuce, the one I had sent back to Vagg with a promise of retribution. The gun was now pointed unwaveringly at my chest.

'You walk light for a big man,' was all I could think of to say.

'Lighter than you could ever imagine, Kid. Now lose the Colt, two fingers with your left hand. You know the drill; toss it over here. You make one false move and this scattergun will cut you in half.'

I did not move, although every muscle in my body was telling me to. Then, very carefully, I did as he asked and tossed the gun to one side.

'And the belly gun.' He motioned to the Rainmaker jammed into my belt, having discarded the shoulder holster when I stripped. I did as I was told but did not toss it as far as the long Colt.

'Frank knows you are up here, Max. He thinks maybe you were among the dead in the canyon, or maybe on the run to Sonora,' I said quietly, my voice even, thinking ahead. Something about that shotgun I had noticed when handling it back in the Red Diamond the night I shot Jimmy the Deuce.

'Frank Vagg's thinking days are over, Santana, only he doesn't know it yet. He has outlived his time. He's too small-minded, fails to see the bigger picture and never thinks beyond the gunmen he hires. I will deal with Frank Vagg now his minder has left and I will control this border. In a few days he will be just a part of it . . . only he will be six feet under it.' He smiled, but the ugly double muzzles with their tightly choked bores still did not waver. 'He lost the gold and he bet on the wrong side of the mountain for the Denver and Rio Grande right of way. Still, San Pedro is a sweet deal. When your Pinkerton friends and the gold have gone, no one will really care what happens down here.'

'That may not be so.'

'It will be so. No one will miss you, Santana. That female you have been pally with: she another agent? Didn't turn out well for the last one, did it? You are just not very lucky with women.'

'I've had my moments.'

'Now you have had your last one, it's time to go, Kid. You have no idea how long I waited for this one moment. Missed you in Wyoming when that bitch moved, but I sure as hell will not miss this time.'

And that was it, right out of nowhere. This man, Max Hadley, had killed my Annie Blue.

There was no rage in me: that had all burned out months before. There was no regret in the sense that

141

regret would have been to deny all of the immense pleasure Annie and I had shared. What was done was done, but I was certain in that one moment in my life that it was not going to end there in that rock-strewn plain with me dead, and Annie not avenged. It was that thinking that saved my life, that mindset that so often held me apart from other hunters of men, seekers of the truths that make us what we are, what we were and what we become. I was not afraid; my mind was as cold and as sharp as a new razor blade. Hadley was the carrier of such a hate that had drawn him to faraway Wyoming to kill me from ambush years after I had, in his mind, done him wrong. He was impatient to kill me but unhurried as to how he went about it, savouring a moment that would live with him forever, or so he believed.

Why is it when some men set out to kill and have you under their gun, they cannot help themselves but try to talk you to death?

It was a mistake that gave me an edge. When I had handled the English shotgun, I had noticed the trigger pull was not light. The original owner, in all probability a game shooter before the barrels had been cropped, preferred the heavier pull on the lightweight gun.

That one piece of information gave me the edge and I used it.

I dived for the Rainmaker fast. I hit the ground hard and rolled to my left, tumbling over several times before settling briefly on my back and firing three quick upward and aimless double action rounds at his big body. If the shotgun had a lighter trigger pull he would have gotten off a shot in my direction, but it didn't and he could not.

My first round hit him in the lower lip; the second took off a chunk of his right ear and the third ploughed into and upwards through his big belly. When he finally discharged the shotgun, it was pointed at his left foot and blew a large hole in his black boot, taking most of his toes with it. I straightened quickly and stood over him. He was trying to speak but his blood-soaked words were indiscernible. The eyes were not filled with the pain I expected to see but with a hate impossible to believe, a vision straight from hell that would haunt me and join the rest of my dark night horses. My immediate thought was to leave him to die long and hard on that mountain, gut shot and paralysed, but Annie Blue would not have approved, so I cocked the piece and shot him through the left eye.

I picked up the shotgun and took half-a-dozen shells from the pocket of his long frock coat and moved from that clearing to a large flat rock a hundred or so yards away from his body. My mouth was dry and my ears ringing from the thunder of the gunshots in that rock-filled enclosure. I would have moved further, but suddenly my legs would not carry me, and I began to tremble, and then to weep. The tears flowed freely. After a while I pulled myself together, extracted the spent shells from my

143

Rainmaker and reloaded it, leaving an empty under the hammer. It was an excellent piece in single or double action. I sat there, thinking quietly of disjointed thoughts: rivers and wolves and spring mornings in a Wyoming breeze, on a grassland littered with wildflowers, and aspen groves filled with bird song. Such thoughts steadied my trembling hands as I went through Hadley's saddlebags and removed a large leather pouch of Mexican gold coins and transferred them to my own. He had undoubtedly removed them from one of the dead mules before we had arrived on the scene. I stripped his horse and turned it loose, knowing one way or another it would find its way back to the Circle V. Then, very tired, I chose a flat rock a hundred yards or so from the body and waited for I know not what . . . some sort of epiphany, maybe?

Nothing happened.

After a little while I noticed a pair of ravens, their black eyes in their black heads eying me, wondering if I was a threat to them this far away from the ranch in the valley by the river from which they had been driven. Smart bird, the raven. Feeling I was not a threat to them, they moved down to lunch on the dead Max Hadley, very much late of Bitter Creek, New Mexico. One sat on his forehead and attacked the bloody wound of his eye socket and the other chose the shot away foot. I smiled to myself: maybe they would meet somewhere in the middle before the coyote, the cougar and bigger raptors were aware of the feast offered them by the dead one-time deputy sheriff of Dry Water, south Texas. This was my Tempest. '*Hell is empty and all of the devils are here . . .*'

I am a well-read man, as Annie would have said of that passing thought.

CHAPTER TWENTY-TWO

TRAIL'S END

By the time I arrived back in San Pedro the following day, it was late afternoon, and Henri met me at the livery. She was pleased to see me and I was pleased that she was pleased.

'We were worried.'

'No need, but thanks just the same,' I said.

'You find Hadley?' she asked quietly.

'Yes, I did. I found him, right enough.'

'And?'

'He will not be coming back.'

'Permanently?'

'Very.'

She looked around carefully and then moved closer to me, allowing me to pull her close and kiss her gently. I stood back and ran my fingers through her hair.

'You smell like your horse and you need a shave,' she said, but did not pull away for a long moment. Then she stepped back, her voice a little above a whisper. 'I am so happy that you are OK. Beaufort said you would be but I was not so sure. You left an angry man, and angry men make mistakes.'

'You are right about that. It was close, but it is now done and a lot of my misery died with him. How are things here?'

'Beaufort has called a meeting and booked a private room at the Drover's. Dinner at eight: that gives you time to wash up, get a shave, change and maybe get an hour's rest. You OK with that?'

'Go tell them I'm back and I won't be late.'

'Yes, boss,' she said with a chuckle. 'I will do just that.'

Then she was gone, leaving with me the scent of her hair in my nostrils and the taste of her lips on mine. *Do detectives ever grow old*, I wondered, *or do they, like old soldiers, just fade away?* I felt very tired, my back ached, my legs were stiff and my ears were still ringing a little from the Rainmaker and the shotgun blast, but I certainly did not feel old.

They were already drinking when I arrived following a bath, a change of clothes and an hour's catnap. Beaufort was seated at the round table with Benbow to his right, Billy Bob Hunt to his left and Henri next to

147

an empty seat, which I assumed, was for me, and had either been Beaufort's or Henri's idea.

'I hear you had a successful hunt, Lucas, and I am glad to hear it.' Beaufort raised his glass, as did the others, and I charged mine and toasted what he considered to be a successful mission. And so it was in most respects. The gold, except for the coins now safely locked in my room, was recovered. Hadley was dead, Vagg's men mostly dead and Billy Bob Hunt was back as one of the highest office holders in the county. But somehow that did not all sit well with me. However, unusually for me, I held my own council on that.

'The Diaz gold left this afternoon with an escort of battle-hardened cavalry sent by the US Marshal's office and with a posse of our people to protect it. I see no reason it will not be delivered safely to San Antonio. Benbow and I will be leaving first thing tomorrow on the Overland and Henri will follow later in the week; apparently she has some unfinished business here.' Beaufort could not resist a wink in my direction.

I ignored the inference but offered him a smile. I liked him very much.

'And Vagg?' I asked quietly. 'What of the old man responsible for the killing and the chaos? All of those bodies in Diablo are on his tally sheet.'

Beaufort nodded his head in the direction of the county sheriff.

'Vagg's about done,' Billy Bob offered, not hiding the delight in his voice. 'His sister has left him cold;

148

run off to New Orleans with her albino bodyguard and took most of his fortune with her. Seems most of his funds and land transactions were tied up in her name. Smart lady, that one; will probably run for public office one day. Even Hector Munro quit: left for Nogales this morning, his voice a little higher but happy to be gone.'

'So that's it?' I asked.

'No real proof against Vagg for any of the shootings. He just sits there with his one manservant, drinking fine wine and chewing on peyote. He's already in his own hell: leave him there, I say. The county will not pursue any charges, but if you boys want to, that will be OK with me.' He looked at me and then at Beaufort.

'You OK with that, Lucas?'

'I am not happy with it, but I will study on it some and get back to you. The man is a killer. He may not have pulled a trigger but he sure enough loaded the guns.'

Beaufort was quiet for a moment, looking from me to Henri and back again before finally deciding to pick up the bell beside his plate. He rang it, and within seconds two waiters from the Drovers were among us, heaping our plates and pouring our wine.

CHAPTER
TWENTY-THREE

THE END GAME

Henri and I watched as the dust from the departing Overland stage settled on the rutted street of San Pedro. I leaned against one of the sidewalk uprights and stacked my pipe, looking into the half-distance somewhere between tomorrow and sundown, wondering just what would be the right thing for me to do to finish this unfinished assignment. I had originally been hired to check out the business of Frank Vagg, and that I had done, but his sitting out on his ranch untouched by the mayhem he had created irritated me. At just about that moment, as I made up my mind what needed doing to end it, Henri drifted up to my side and leaned against me. I put my arm around her shoulders and squeezed.

'You are going out to see him, aren't you?'

It was not really a question but more a statement of fact, probably known to her long before I ever reached that same conclusion.

'I guess I will have to.'

'Will it help? He is a mean, duplicitous man and nothing you can do about it, but go if you must. I will understand. But be careful: he is a wounded animal in many ways and probably looking for a place and a way to die that will mean something to somebody, if not to himself.'

I placed my unlit pipe in my pocket and kissed her lightly on the cheek. 'I will be careful.'

There was nothing more to say. I winked at her and crossed the street slowly to the livery stable and one more ride on the Morgan.

It was a little after midday when I rode into the deserted front yard of the Circle V. The only signs of life were two ponies standing hip shod in the large pole corral, their tails busy brushing away the horse flies, and a thin trail of smoke drifting from the cook-shack's stone chimney. Miguel, Vagg's manservant, was asleep on the porch rocker. He was not the man he had been: his shirt was soiled and sweat stained, his pants creased and dirty and he sported several days' growth on his dark face. He was snoring and tobacco juice slipped from his lower lip. I kicked the chair hard and he sat bolt upright, then, ignoring me, slipped back into the chair. I kicked again, harder this time.

'Can I help you, *señor*?' His words were slurred and he stank of cheap whiskey.

'I came to see Mr Vagg. Please tell him I am here.'

'Mr Vagg is not at home.'

'Go tell him anyway,' I said.

He thought about that for a long moment, got unsteadily to his feet and went into the house, staggering a little.

I waited on his return; it was only a matter of minutes.

'Mr Vagg will be happy to see you. Follow me, please.'

I brushed past him, telling him I knew the way, and he stepped to one side. I watched as he sank back onto the rocker, his head dropping forward and his chin hitting his chest with an audible crunch. Within seconds he was snoring again.

It seemed to me that Frank Vagg had diminished considerably in size. He was seated in a wicker wheelchair in front of a table littered with the remains of a breakfast, a half-empty bottle of whiskey and two glasses. His white-shirted shoulders and lap were covered in plaid wool blankets, the shoulders and hands hidden in the warmth of their depths. His only visible skin was the skull-like pallid face, with its goatee wisp of a beard and the lids covering piercing black eyes. His large-brimmed Panama hat rested on the tops of his large ears. He gave the appearance of a decaying heap of tattered brush waiting for the south Texas wind to blow him away. He studied me for some moments before indicating the chair opposite him with a nod of his head.

'Take a seat. Smoke if you want; there are cigars on the side table.' His voice was thin, rasping, almost a whisper.

I shook my head and took out my pipe, but did not light it.

'Nothing to say? You are not usually a man short on words, Santana.'

In truth, in that moment I was uncertain and not sure of what I wanted to say, although I had gone over the meeting many times on my ride out to the Circle V.

'I knew you would come eventually, either to gloat or to arrest me. Which is it to be?'

'Neither, actually,' I said.

'What else is there?' he said, puzzled by my reply.

'I wanted to ask you a question. Just the one.'

'And that would be?'

'Why?'

'Why, what?' he said.

'Why did you do what you did? Why did you orchestrate the death or displacement of so many? You didn't need the money; you had a fine ranch here, a business below the border well out of sight or sphere of interference from federal law enforcement, a tame sheriff, wealth and power plenty enough for one man. Why endanger that?'

'Maybe I don't like Texas or Texans. They have an attitude of which I do not approve.'

'Texans are Texans. Men of Texas are no different from you or me,' I smiled, and could see that it irritated him.

'You think you are a smart man, Santana, but you really don't know a lot about people, people with money. We got our money because we wanted it and when we get it we want just a little more. We are acquisitive. We collect money; we invest. It's what we do with the money we get: we use it to make more. You yourself make a little money if you are good at what you do and I guess you steal a little on the side. You are as corrupt as you consider me to be: you just do it on a pennyante level, is all.'

I thought of the gold I had transferred from Max Hadley's saddlebag to my own. So I stole from a thief; did that make me a bad person? Vagg may have been close there and although I ignored it, it was something to think about another time.

'Your current employer, the Pinkerton Agency, is not entirely blameless. You work for the rich, the railroad barons and a discredited, bankrupt government. Were you in on the raid that blew Jesse James' mother and kid brother to oblivion, or are your hands clean?'

I ignored the comment, although, then again, there was some truth in what he said. 'But yours was a senseless gamble,' I pressed on. 'Had you got a hold of the Mexican gold, the army would have been down on you and turned this county upside-down within days and you with it. Your gamble on the railroad: the Denver and Rio Grande was never coming this way. It made no sense. Whoever fed you that information was no friend of yours.'

His cheeks flushed, a startling pink against the whiteness of his skin. Anger: the great betrayer.

'You don't know that, you cannot know that.'

'Your sister, did she leave a forwarding address?'

'Shut your dirty mouth, Santana. You would never understand; you are just a small change gunman, a thief and a liar.'

I sat back in my chair and tamped my pipe, lit it and looked over the smoke at the dry stick of the man I had been hired to investigate. 'You don't really know why, do you, Frank? Your sister has run off with your money and her albino bodyguard, your men are either dead or on the run, you are broke and alone and you have no idea yourself as to the why of any of it.'

Frank Vagg looked at me long and hard. Then a faint smile and a glint burned in the obsidian black eyes, a glimmer that seemed to gather in the darkness of his inner thoughts. He tried to chuckle but it rasped and rattled around inside his chest and came out as a dry cough. I waited: Frank Vagg was a very sick man.

'You consider yourself to be a well-read man, Santana, and are happy to quote Shakespeare when it suits you. Well, so am I. Consider these words: "Life's but a walking shadow, a poor player that struts and frets his hour upon the stage and then is heard no more. It is a tale told by an idiot, full of sound and fury signifying nothing." Macbeth. Now, you think on that as the answer to your question in the few seconds you have left to fret and strut.'

The revolver had been hidden in the folds of the blanket covering his skinny legs. Now it was cocked and pointed at my chest and there was not a damned thing I could do about it.

'Time to say goodbye.' He fixed his pale eyes upon me, the muzzle of the Colt resting on the table between us and clearly pointing in my direction with hammer back, his bony finger white upon the trigger.

A slight pop, a muffled report from somewhere behind me. A look of anger on his distorted face. A growing, flowerlike pattern of dark red on the front of his pristine white shirt. His eyes fixed behind me, anger replaced by fear. His fingers relaxed, and the gun settled gently upon the tabletop then, a second popping sound and a third eye leaked blood as his head snapped back. A cloud of feathers drifted by my head, and I could smell the stink of black powder and the scorching odour of burning cloth. Then Henri Larsson walked past me, my smoking nickel-plated .45 Derringer in one hand and a smouldering cushion in the other. She dropped that onto the floor at my feet. I tipped the last of Vagg's wine over it, causing the feathers to hiss and steam.

I stared at her and then back at the dead man.

'And the cushion?'

'I did not want to awaken the help,' she said quietly.

'You followed me,' I said.

'How observant of you.'

I looked hard at the little .45 she had fired to such

156

devastating effect into the frail body of Frank Vagg. 'I didn't know female agents were permitted to carry,' were the only words I had for her.

'We are not. I could be fired for this, but what the hell, I found it in your room. . . .'

I took the warm piece gently from her trembling hand and dropped it into my jacket pocket. 'Fair shooting for such a little gun,' I said.

'I just pointed and fired is all. Lucky I didn't hit you.'

'Indeed, thank you.'

'I hope it was worth the effort,' she said very quietly.

It was there again, the vaguest hint of laughter in her voice . . . or was it just the satisfaction, the relief of an outcome reached that could have ended badly for me had she not followed me from San Pedro? I could not be sure.

'I will make it so,' I said.

It was all very straight forward after that. I signed the papers for Billy Bob Hunt, describing how I had shot Frank Vagg dead as he threatened me with a revolver when I confronted him with the possibility of his arrest because of his suspected involvement in the killing of the Mexican soldiers and the harassment of the homesteaders on the eastern side of his boundary. The old sheriff noted it as being an act of self-defence and the circuit judge signed off on it. Then, with his best wishes, and after informing Beaufort of our plans by telegraph, we hit the road, riding the Overland to Dallas and the iron rails north to Wyoming.

EPILOGUE

Thoughtfully, Jesse Overlander had replaced the swing seat upon which Annie Blue had taken the .44.40 round that had been meant for me, with a newly constructed wood frame and a lovely woven canvas seat patterned with wildflowers sewn together by his sister. He had moved the seat so that it faced east one way and west the other, and I was reminded of a line from Walt Whitman, the civil war poet: '*Keep your face always toward the sunshine and the shadows will form behind you.*' I did not think Overlander had ever read Whitman, but I could have been wrong about that, as I had been about so many things over the past two years.

Needless to say, but Henri fell in love with Wildcat at first glance. It was that golden Wyoming time of the year and the shadows that had surrounded us over the last month or so dissipated quickly, like the wood smoke from our fire lifted by the ever-gentle breeze. Bart took an instant shine to her, and I often found them up by Willard's Rocks, dressing Annie Blue's grave with wildflowers. There was nothing morbid about their being there; it was simply a gentle homage to a past now shared.

Sometimes I joined them for an evening pipe after a trek around my extended boundary, grown a thousand acres courtesy of the Mexican gold found in Max Hadley's saddle-bags. Yes, Max crossed my mind from time to time, and I pictured his bleaching bones hidden in a dry wash to the south of San Pedro. I saw in my mind's eye the black ravens flying high once again among the rocky crags above the Circle V. Only once did I refer to the shooting of Frank Vagg when, one early evening, I saw her on the porch seat gazing out into nothingness, the thousand yard stare of the weary trooper. Seeing only her own pain and reflection in an event she had little control over, a regret I could not share it with her. I told her it was always like that: taking a life in any circumstances was not something she would ever forget. I also told her that by killing Vagg, a very sick man, and in saving my life she had done us both a great service. I hope that gave her some comfort, but only time will tell.

It was a gentle, even romantic time for the both of us and for my friends in Peaceful, but I wondered on some of the darker midnight evenings sitting on the stoop, alone with my pipe while Henrietta slept warm in our bed, just how long it would last. How long would it be before Joshua Beaufort or Jacob Benbow came calling and I would saddle up and once again ride hard to the sound of gunfire? In moments like those, Poe's words would come to me: '*Once upon a midnight dreary, while I pondered weak and weary . . .*' But I cast them aside; the San Pedro ravens were happy and content, so why should I not be? Sometimes I believe that I may be too well read.